acts of
REDEMPTION

ELEANOR ALDRICK

Acts of Redemption

Copyright © 2020 by Eleanor Aldrick

Cover Design: Sinfully Seductive Designs
Interior Formatting: Sinfully Seductive Designs

FIRST EDITION

ISBN: 978-1-7345272-4-7

10 9 8 7 6 5 4 3 2 1

For the survivors.

To all of the women who've faced adversity and overcome it despite the odds. This book is for you.

"I am proud of the woman I am today, because I went through one hell of a time becoming her."

-author unknown

This book contains mature language, incidents of domestic violence, and steamy love scenes.

With that said, this book also contains female empowerment and a happily ever after.

Enjoy!

NO ONE'S IN THE ROOM – JESSIE REYEZ

THE FRAGILE – NINE INCH NAILS

YOU SHOULD SEE ME IN A CROWN –BILLIE EILISH

BLOOD//WATER – GRANDSON

NO JUDGEMENT – NIALL HORAN

LAY YOUR HEAD ON ME – MAJOR LAZER FEAT. MARCUS
MUMFORD

BURY ME FACE DOWN – GRANDSON

DOWNTOWN - MAJICAL CLOUDZ

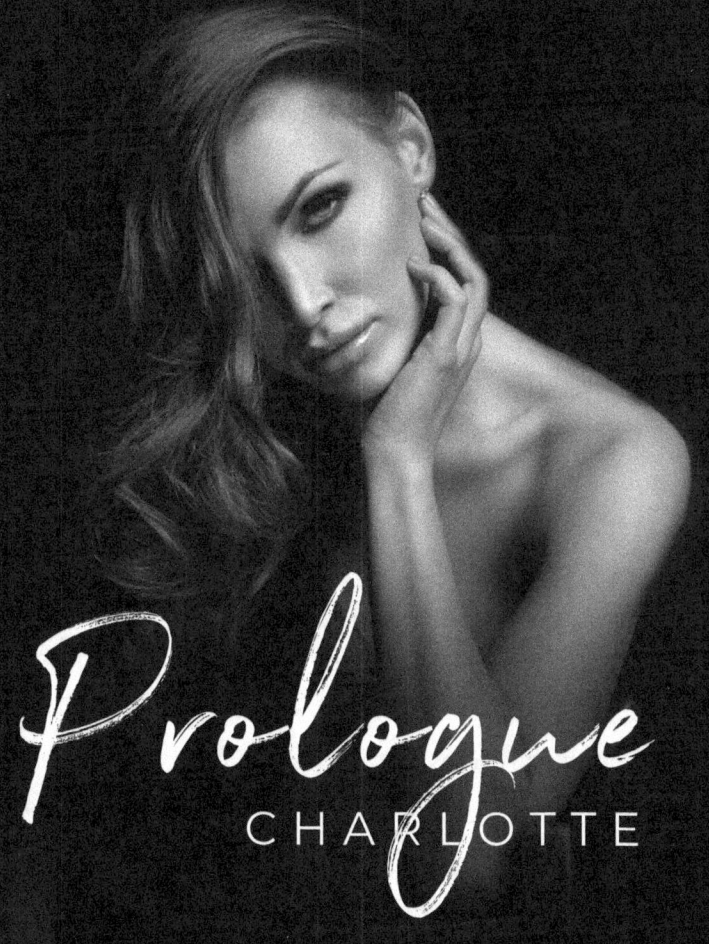

Prologue
CHARLOTTE

"You worthless *cunt*."

A shove to my chest has my head flying backward, hitting the hardwood floor and releasing a loud echo into the conveniently empty room.

It's always empty. That's the way he likes it. No one to hear me cry. No one to see my tears.

"You should be kissing my feet, thanking me for everything I've given you." He crouches down onto the floor, breathing the words onto my neck as he pulls my head back, forcing me to look him in the eyes. "Remember, Charlotte... you are nothing without me."

His spittle lands on my face, but I don't flinch. Any movement on my part would only bring on more pain. *More torture.*

He finally releases my hair and begins to pace back and forth.

Motionless, like a broken rag doll, I remain on the ground—not wanting to draw any more attention to myself. He's silent for what feels like an eternity, and I pray it's a sign that he's ready to move on for the night.

Prayer. A fucking novelty, really.

I squeeze my eyes shut and give it one last shot.

God, if you're out there, please make this torture stop. Please end my pain.

A tear rolls down my cheek. The cold salty liquid stings as it reaches my split lip, reminding me I'm still here. Still living this hellish nightmare.

His steel-tipped cowboy boot connects with a punishing blow to my ribs, making me instinctively roll into the fetal position and shut my eyes.

"Ah, ah, ahh. Keep those pretty little eyes of yours open. I'm not done with you yet." His strong hands uncurl me from my position before reaching up for my nape, forcing me once again to face him.

Looking up at him, I see nothing but hatred and rage in his eyes, causing something in me to finally snap.

"*Why*? Why the fuck did you marry me if you hate me so much? If you won't believe me and just think the worst of me...

then why?" my voice cracks—just like my soul, which is shattered beyond repair.

"Oh, Charlotte. Don't you see? You're my little doll. My plaything." He *tsks* as he shakes his head. "Every man of importance needs a trophy by his side."

This sick fuck. He never loved me. This is all a game to him. It's all a show.

I'm not a person, just a possession.

"Ah, that look on your face tells me you finally understand. Good. Maybe now you'll stay in line." He walks toward the door, but turns around before leaving me to clean up his mess. "You'll be getting new security detail, and no more whoring around with the staff. Those legs only open up for me."

And with those parting words, he's gone—leaving me a crumpled mess on the floor.

I roll on to my back and stare at the ceiling with its intricate design and gold leaf gilding. I wonder how many tragedies it's seen. I bet mine is nothing new, just one of many.

A tale of woe as old as time.

We are at a gala among the Dallas elite, yet no one will bat a lash when I reenter the room with a split lip and a slight limp in my gait.

Don't ask, don't tell. That's their *modus operandi.* Lord knows there's nothing more uncouth than showing genuine emotion or concern.

I live in a world of fraud. Everyone and everything is fake. Plastic. Superficial.

Closing my eyes, I pick myself up, vowing to never let myself fall apart. Never let myself conform to their ways.

I fluff my unconventionally long black hair—a silent fuck you to the sea of blond that surrounds me—and straighten my dress.

Giving myself a mental peptalk before I reenter the world of dolls, I put on a smile.

Charlotte Annabelle Montgomery, this does not define you. You are *worthy, you* are *special, and you* will *survive this.*

Fuck anyone who stands in your way.

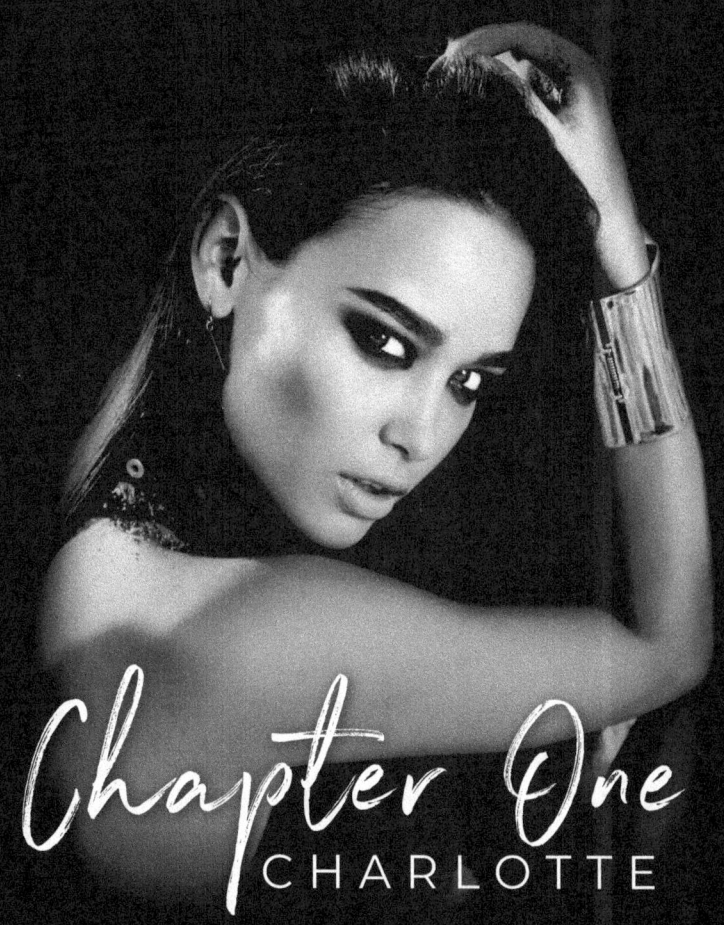

Chapter One

CHARLOTTE

Coffee. The only delectable thing I'm looking forward to this morning.

Its rich aroma pulls me from the depths of my room and into the kitchen where the beautiful Sandra is whipping up breakfast. She's been a godsend. The only person I can count on aside from myself in this godforsaken world of falsity.

And though I would trust Sandra with most things, there are still parts of my life I'd like to keep to myself.

Secrets are demons not to be shared. They lurk in the shadows, waiting to detonate and obliterate everyone and everything in their wake.

I've made that mistake before and paid dearly for it. *Never again.*

"Morning, Mrs. Rutherford. Would you like your egg white omelette now?" Sandra smiles at me while holding out a glorious cup of caffeine. Her rosy cheeks and beautiful silver hair make her the perfect Mrs. Claus doppelgänger, adding to her already likable personality.

"No thank you, Sandra. And please, just call me Charlotte."

Sandra's previously joyous face puckers as she looks at our surroundings before shaking her head repeatedly. "Oh, no. Mr. Rutherford has given me specific instructions. I'm never to address you so casually."

She spins around and busies herself with the already impeccably clean kitchen.

Spinning on my heels, I blow out a breath as I make my way back to my room. Figures the warden of my life would prevent anyone from getting close to me. Even my dear Sandra is off-limits.

I'm about to close the door behind me when my husband's secretary buzzes through the intercom. "Mrs. Rutherford? Your new detail is here. The senator wanted you to meet with them immediately upon their arrival."

I press my forehead against the door and groan.

"What was that, Mrs. Rutherford?"

"Nothing. I'll be there in a minute. Thank you, Michaela."

I silence any further questioning by pushing the white button on the panel by the door. For a few brief moments, I'd forgotten about last night's ordeal. Ridiculous because my ribs still bear the imprint of Preston's boots.

Placing my mug on the nightstand, I stare toward my walk-in closet, contemplating throwing on a pair of sweats instead of the conservative black dress I know Preston would approve of.

Snickering, I pull on the matching gray sweater and pant set. I fancy it up by scrunching up the sleeves, throwing on my five inch Manolo Blahnik, and popping on a bright pink gloss to my lips, still bruised from the night before.

Content with my fashion choices for the day, I exit the room with my head held high. Let the bastard make a scene in front of people. Joke will be on him.

A new detail means that whoever is assigned to me will watch me like a hawk for the first couple of months until they let their guard down. This doesn't bode well for Preston and his alter ego.

As I turn the corner, I see Sandra stealing glances into the parlor. *Interesting.* She's not usually one to butt her head into business other than hers.

The corner of my mouth lifts into a smirk, my right eyebrow cocking involuntarily. "What's so entertaining?" I whisper as I reach Sandra's side.

She jolts up, no doubt startled. "Mm—Mrs. Rutherford. Your new detail is here." Her face is pale, no longer holding any semblance of the rosiness I saw just moments ago.

My brows come together and my smile sours. Turning toward the sitting area, I see what's caused Sandra's concern.

Holy shit.

The men in the other room are drop-dead gorgeous. Like something straight out of a GQ magazine. Wearing tailored suits that fit their body perfectly, there is no doubt that nothing but taught and tantalizing muscle lies underneath.

My eyes travel back and forth between the two men before me, and I'm about to push my mouth shut when I hear someone clearing their throat to my right.

Lord, help me. How did I miss him?!

If I thought the other two were GQ models, this one was sent straight from heaven. A deity walking this earth.

My eyes narrow as I study his face further. He looks familiar. But surely... *No. No. This cannot be happening.*

Like a freight train slamming into an unsuspecting vehicle, the memories assault me one by one.

His thick black hair, chiseled jaw, and piercing hazel eyes as rich as the timbre of his voice are enough to haunt my dreams for eternity.

Closing my eyes, I take a centering breath before entering the room. If I'm to survive the next six months I need to present the mother of all facades.

"Good morning, gentlemen. I'm Charlotte Rutherford." Stealing a quick glance toward tall, dark and handsome, I check to see if he's recognized me. I intentionally omitted my maiden name, and it's been decades since he's last seen me, so luck is on my side... at least I hope it is.

"Good morning, ma'am." The deity approaches me, not a hint of recognition in his beautiful eyes. "Name is Aiden Moretti. I'll be the lead assigned to you, however, Titus here will cover for me when I'm not on duty." He points toward one of the other men in the room who must be Titus.

Shifting my gaze back toward Aiden, I have to ask, "Has my husband met with you and your team, personally?"

"No, ma'am. We met with Michaela." After a beat, Aiden arches a brow. "Is there a problem?"

"Am I to believe Michaela gave you an itinerary and breakdown of my daily schedule, routines, and social engagements?" Completely ignoring his question, I power on. There's no way in hell I'm going to give him even an inkling of trouble in paradise. The last thing I need is for him to report back that I'm in some sort of trouble.

"Yes, ma'am." His tone is flat, lacking any emotion. But his eyes—those eyes—they tell me the truth. He hasn't missed the fact that I haven't answered his question and his eyes are trained on my bruised lip.

"Great, so you're aware of my meeting with the mayor's wife this afternoon. I have a couple of stops before I meet her for lunch. I'd like to leave in about thirty minutes."

"That won't be a problem, Mrs. Rutherford." His hazel eyes narrow, but no further comment follows.

Giving him a nod, I turn on my heels and head back to my room, needing to pick up my bag and the donations I'd compiled the last couple of weeks.

I'm about to reach my door when I hear heavy steps behind me. Whirling around, I almost run straight into a brick of chest. Slowly lifting my gaze upward, I'm met with the richest hazel eyes I've ever seen. Like deep pools of cashmere, I want to dive right in and envelop myself in their warmth.

"Ma'am, is everything okay?" His deep voice cuts into my thoughts and breaks me out of my trance.

"Yes, I'm not sure why you're following me. There's no need to follow me inside of the home." My brows furrow and my forehead crinkles. "This level of surveillance is unnecessary here."

"Mr. Rutherford begs to differ." That's it. That's all he gives me.

Well, shit. This is next-level smothering. Not only does Preston dictate who I can and cannot talk to, but he's now having me followed in my own home? If I felt like a prisoner before, now I'm definitely at Rikers.

Closing my eyes, I take in a deep breath. *Abort. Abort. Abort.* Huge mistake. Now all I'll be able to think of is the smell of Aiden's delicious scent of bergamot and cedarwood.

The scent takes me back to my childhood, where I was always the third wheel. Mother would never let Clarabelle go on dates alone, and it was little ol' me that got to witness her making out with the man of my dreams. Over and over again.

A hand to my shoulder startles me into opening my eyes. Once again, I'm looking into those beautiful pools of hazel, but now they're riddled with concern.

"You okay?" Two words. Oh, if he only knew.

"Yes." I sigh before smiling and shaking my head. "Well then, if that's what Mr. Rutherford wants, then that is what Mr. Rutherford gets." With a demure huff, I turn and enter my room to retrieve my bag and the tube of gloss I'd left on the vanity.

Looking in the mirror one last time, I see that Aiden is standing inside my room. Our eyes meet and I swear it's as if he's looking into my soul. The man can see me. Me and the skeletons I've shoved in my closet.

I clear my throat, needing to break the tension that's suddenly filled the air. "Right, well. We should get going."

I'm about to step past Aiden when his strong callused hand reaches out and grabs my arm, sending a current of electricity shooting straight through to my core. "Charlotte, is there anything I should know about?"

My eyes begin to tingle, the warning I need to snap me out of this weakened state. I will not cry in front of this man, nor will I let on about what dirty secrets I hold.

"Nothing you haven't been briefed on. Now if you'll please let me go, we have places to be, people to see, and things to do. If you'd like to help, you can carry those boxes out to the car. It will be our first stop."

Donning a sincere smile, I pray he lets it go. The last thing I need is for Preston to catch a whiff of my history with Aiden.

We'd have much bigger problems than his getting fired, and that's not a risk I'm willing to take.

Chapter Two
AIDEN

That tiny woman is infuriating. She might be small, but what she lacks in height, she makes up for in defiance. I know she's holding something back. I can see it in her eyes.

Behind those big brown eyes, I see fear. I've seen it one too many times in my thirty-nine years not to recognize it. Being in the Navy, you see it every damn day. Some disguise it better than others, but if you know where and how to look, it's as clear as day.

How the fuck am I supposed to protect her if she won't let me know what she fears. Or better yet, *who*?

I tip back my rocks glass, letting the amber liquid drip down my throat and warm my chilly disposition.

"What's got you in a mood?" Ren, my little brother asks from across the library.

He is one of the five founding members of our private security firm, WRATH Securities. What started out as a small hometown operation run by childhood friends has now grown into a nationwide enterprise, providing services to some of the most prominent figures in our country.

We all have our roles to play. William is the entrepreneur, he's the one behind all the paperwork; Ren is a tech guru, the man can hack into any system, regardless of who's built it; Titus has investigative skills that could make the pope shudder in fear; Hudson is our money guy, he oversees all the financials; and lastly, myself—As a former Navy SEAL, I'm the chief of security, usually ending up with the higher profile cases.

And right at this very moment, we're all gathered at William and Bella's home for their Sunday dinner. A new tradition started by my daughter in an effort to keep our group together as everyone grows into their own lives.

"He's always in a mood." Titus ribs. "He's probably still messed up from those blows to his head."

"Ha, ha. Hilarious. Keep joking and I'll make sure you end up back in Arkansas." I give him a poignant stare and he calms the fuck down, knowing I'm not joking. About a year ago he did a job in some tiny town where his usually bountiful supply of women was cut down to zero. It's safe to say he hated it there.

In all sincerity, I know they still worry. It's been a long six months since I've recovered from a brain injury. Apparently multiple bullet wounds and trauma to the head left me with a much shorter fuse than normal.

When I found out that William, my thirty-two-year-old business partner and close friend was dating my eighteen-year-old daughter... Well, let's just say I wasn't a bowl of sunshine and rainbows.

For the past couple of months, I've been working on rebuilding the relationship with my daughter and getting my home life situated. Bella is now engaged to William, and my two eight-year-old boys are home, where they belong.

"You can be in whatever mood you want whenever you want, as long as it doesn't interfere with the wedding." William, my business partner, friend and soon to be son-in-law chimes in. "You'll need to be in top form for the fittings and wedding preparations. Don't think you're off the hook just because you haven't been around. Make no mistake, we want you involved in every excruciating process."

I chuckle, "Unless you want to end up with lime green tablecloths or ribeyes for a dinner entrée, I suggest you leave me out of the planning. I'm good for writing checks, though. Isn't that what the father of the bride usually does, anyway?"

"Yes, but if the rest of us are being dragged into planning the festivities, then so are you. No exceptions just because you're Daddy Warbucks." Titus raises his glass in my direction.

"Hudson, you're the only one who hasn't put their two cents in. Everything okay?" William looks at Hudson expectantly. He's usually the talkative one in our bunch, but tonight he's a borderline recluse.

"What? Oh, yeah. Everyone has to share in the misery of wedding planning. No exceptions." Hudson gives a quick nod before his eyes return to the window. Something's definitely up. I make a mental note to ask him about it later.

"Aiden, how's the new live-in nanny working out? You know the boys are welcome to stay with us anytime you need help." William's sincerity shines through his eyes, and despite everything we've all been through, I take comfort in knowing I can always count on our crew. I really couldn't have asked for a better group of friends.

Bella had been helping me care for the boys since the age of fifteen when their mother died. And when I suffered my injury, William took them all in, helping Bella with all the duties she'd been undertaking on her own.

Bastard did a better job than I'd been doing, that's for sure. Not that I'll ever admit it.

"Thanks, brother, but I think we've got it handled. Bella's done too much for far too long. I fear I've robbed too much of her adolescence with all of the responsibilities I laid on her. I think the new nanny and I can manage."

It's true. That woman is a powerhouse. She's like the grandmother I never had, doting on the boys as if they were her own flesh and blood.

"So, how's the new job going?" Ren's sincere question has Titus snickering into his glass.

"The way he dotes on the woman, you'd think she was his long-lost love."

I roll my eyes and shake my head at Titus' dumb-ass remark. "She's our charge. The most high profile one we've had yet. I'd hate to fuck up our reputation because little miss perfect doesn't want to give me all the facts." Bringing my rocks glass to my lips, I take a long sip before continuing. "I think she's hiding something, but I'm not quite sure what it is. Have we identified why the Texas Rangers were discharged as their private security?"

Typically, senators have a government-assigned protective detail. In Texas, that responsibility lands on the Texas Ranger Division.

William runs his hand across his face. "Yeah, about that..."

I'm not liking the sound of this.

"Did something not make it into the briefing? Something I should know about?" I raise a brow, waiting for the proverbial bomb to drop.

"It's all on the down low. Very hush-hush and definitely not in any official record. We got word that the senator was accusing one of the rangers of having illicit interactions with his wife."

"*Illicit?* Does she have a drug problem?" I spit out a wild theory because there is no way that little spitfire was having an affair. She doesn't strike me as the type.

But then what the hell do I know. My late wife had been having an affair for years and I hadn't the slightest clue.

"No. The senator accused them of having extramarital relations."

Fuck.

"Is there a reason I wasn't informed of this sooner?" My entire body turns rigid, completely uncomfortable with my new reality. I'm in charge of protecting a cheater. A *fucking* cheater.

The men look at each other, but only Ren has the balls to say anything to my face. "Look, we know how you feel about

17

infidelity. We didn't want it to taint your performance. Like you said, it's the highest profile case we've landed, and we wanted our best on the job."

"I'm flattered, really." Grumbling, I lift my hand to my hair, running it through and pulling at the ends. "But seriously, this is something I should've been informed about."

"Hey, maybe she did nothing wrong, and the senator is the one who's a jealous fuck. Don't tarnish the image of your perfect little princess just yet." Titus shoots me a toothy grin.

"She's not my anything so cut that shit right out." I stand to head outside, needing some space from these men. They're family, but family can definitely get annoying. "I expect the entire roster of her previous detail to be in my inbox tomorrow morning. I'll want to talk to them myself."

I get a unanimous '*Mhm*,' and though we all hold equal rank, I know they'll put in the appropriate request and make it happen.

I need to get to the bottom of her secrets. However disturbing they might be.

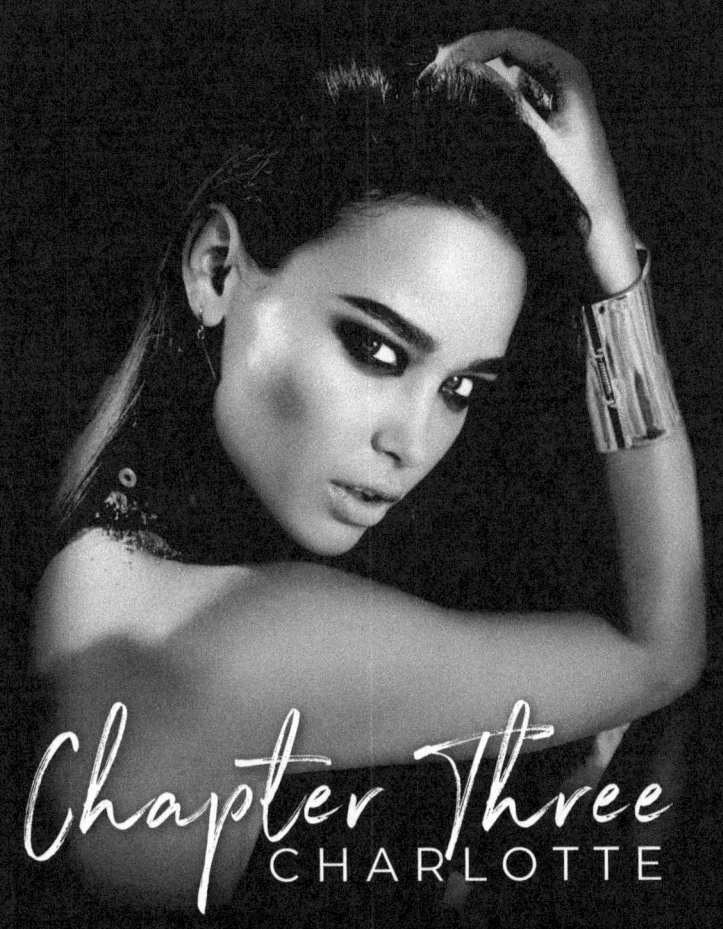

Chapter Three
CHARLOTTE

He's different. I can feel it. Something's happened, and it's changed the way he looks at me.

"Everything okay?" I try to temper my voice, not wanting to give away any emotion. Lord knows he doesn't show any. *Ever.*

"Yes." His focus remains straight ahead. I'm not even graced with his cold cashmere eyes. *Has he figured out who I am?*

We're on our way to the women's shelter. *Ironic, I know.* If I can't escape my reality, then I'll do everything in my power to help others escape theirs. Volunteering once a week helps soothe the chasm in my heart and helps me keep going. Keep pushing this image of the perfect southern belle, the perfect wife, and the epitome of strength and elegance when I feel anything but.

I throw my head back against the headrest of the SUV we're in. My hand falls out of my lap and accidentally brushes Aiden's arm, instantly sending tingles coursing through my body. Turning my head, I see he's staring right at me, those intense eyes narrowing before he removes his hand and refocuses his attention to the front of the vehicle.

Ugh. This is going to be a long day. I close my eyes again, refusing to let myself relive the angst of my childhood.

"Why?" His deep voice has my eyes shooting open. Surprised at the sudden question, but I'm not sure what he's asking.

Turning my body toward him, my brows furrow, "Why what?"

"Why are you choosing to volunteer at a women's shelter? There are plenty of charities or nonprofits that could use exposure from the senator's wife. Why this shelter?"

His question makes my stomach churn, sending bile crawling up my throat. Trying to school my face, I give him a generic answer, not at all having any semblance of truth. "It was one of the first organizations on the list provided to me by Michaela."

I turn my head, refusing to let him see my eyes. There's no doubt he'd be able to sniff out my lies, and I'm no fool. If he catches on to the fact that things aren't what they seem between Preston and me...

Even though I'm no longer looking at him, I can feel his burning stare. After what feels like an eternity, he finally releases a low huff—showing more emotion than I've seen from him these past couple of days.

"We're here." He exits the vehicle first, offering his hand as I scoot to the edge of the seat.

Placing my hand in his, that pesky jolt resurfaces and I can't help but look up into his eyes. They're staring right at me, narrowed with something swimming behind the irises. What I would give to dive in and swim through his thoughts. *Does he see me? The real me?*

A throat clearing to the right has our staring match breaking, and I see Titus looking at Aiden with a raised brow.

Right. That's my cue to get moving. Both men flank me as I enter the facility. The smell of sterile cleaning solutions invades my nose, but despite the coldness of the environment, there's a warmth to the place.

Hope. It's here in spades. You can feel it in the air and see it on the faces of the women who inhabit these four walls. They know that despite the darkness of their past, from this point forward things will be different. It will be a struggle, sure, but none of it will compare to the hell they've just survived.

The women here are warriors. Every single one of them.

A burning sensation hits me straight in the gut. *Jealousy.* My hand instinctively covers my stomach as I suck in a deep breath, needing to reign in my emotions.

As if on instinct, Aiden's hand lands on the small of my back, a questioning look in his eyes. Despite the expression, no words flow from his lips—I for one am grateful for that. There's no way I could respond to any of them with truth.

I give him a nod as I straighten myself out, letting him know that I'm fine. His hand drops from my body and I instantly feel the

21

loss of his warmth. Needing to shake this sensation, I quickly locate Meredith, the facility's director.

"Morning, beautiful." A genuine smile spreads across her lips. She's the closest thing to a real friend I have, and I cherish our time together dearly. "I see you have new security." Her gaze travels up and down the length of Aiden's body, who's standing stoically behind me.

And even though she's my friend, at this very moment I want to gouge out her eyes. Closing my eyes, I shake my head. These are no thoughts a married woman should have. He is *not* mine. *Never has been and never will be.*

"Yes." No further explanation follows. Despite our closeness, I would never divulge the secrets of my marriage. She's a trained professional, and there's no doubt in my mind that she'd be able to spot the issues a mile away.

"Alright then. Shall we head to the computer room? The girls are all waiting." She motions toward the hallway to the right.

I've been teaching computer lessons, giving the women the basic knowledge to hold down an entry level administrative position. It's part of the program here, not only offering shelter, but empowering women to be able to provide for themselves and their families.

Smiling as I follow Meredith I can't help but giggle to myself. I have a feeling that today's lesson will be difficult for the ladies. Not because what I'll be covering is complex. Nope. It's the eye candy I've brought with me that will be their demise.

But hey, I can't blame them. After all, he was the subject of my fantasies all throughout my adolescence.

And now, the real struggle is keeping him out of the ones in my present.

Exiting the Escalade, we make our way toward the house when I see my sister's sleek black Mercedes in the roundabout. My steps falter and I know I'm about to land face-first into the asphalt when a set of strong hands land on either side of my hips, fingers digging into my flesh in an almost bruising grasp.

My breath halts and the air around me freezes. Slowly, Aiden rights me, our eyes finding each other once again and a million words are spoken with that one glance.

"Better watch your step, or my perfect little princess will lose her image of perfection." The corner of his lips lift into an almost unperceivable smirk. But I know him, and I see it as clear as day.

My cheeks flush at the term of endearment—if you can call it that—it's one he's called me since my childhood. *So he does remember.*

A sense of relief and sorrow come over me as I know he's about to revisit a ghost from his past. The way things ended between him and my sister were *not* pretty. They dated pretty hot and heavy and when my father caught wind of how serious things were getting, he made Clara cut things off, stating that even though Aiden came from old money, he'd never be good enough for his daughter. He was an immigrant's son, and that just wouldn't do for the Montgomery name.

I roll my eyes at the memory. If I'd been the one dating Aiden, I would've told my father right where he could have shoved it.

The closer we get to the front door, the sooner this shit show will unfold. There's no way he'd know that the car in the driveway belongs to Clarabelle, so I feel inclined to warn him.

"Aiden, Clara—"

"Is inside." A small smile graces his lips as my mouth parts open.

"How did you know?"

"What kind of protective detail would I be if I didn't know everyone and everything potentially affecting your safety?" His face is back to being the impassive, impenetrable fortress, and I can't help but feel the loss once more.

"Right." My lips roll in as I take a deep breath. Preparing myself for what, I'm not sure. All I know is that this is going to be interesting.

And by interesting, I mean painful. *Very painful.*

Chapter Four

AIDEN

I should have known that eventually I'd have to face Clara. As soon as the file landed on my desk declaring Charlotte Rutherford Montgomery as my new charge, I knew my world was about to take a turn for the interesting.

I've known who she is from day one. Give me some credit. I'm a SEAL. There isn't much that gets past me.

I'd been leaving it up to the little princess to bring up our history. Not that it really had much to do with her, but more her sister, really. Her sister and her prick of a father.

The last time I saw Charlotte she was just a lanky little girl, but I will never forget her eyes as they watched me leave their home for the last time. I could tell she didn't share the same beliefs as her father, and I've never blamed her for what that family put me through.

The little squirt always had more common sense and ethics than her sister possessed in one of her well-manicured fingers. Did I love Clarabelle? No. Was she hot as fuck? Yes.

But can you really blame me? I was nineteen and thinking with my cock. Any boy my age would've been in full lust with Clara.

The double doors open to the French Chateau and the white-haired Sandra stands there, her rosy cheeks a welcoming sight in this otherwise frigid environment. Aside from Sandra and Charlotte, everyone else acts as if they lack a pulse. And that's saying something coming from me, the honorary king of stoicism.

"It's about ti—" Clara's words get cut off as she sees exactly who's entering the sitting area.

"Hello, sister. To what do I owe the pleasure." Charlotte, ever the picture of manners, doesn't acknowledge Clara's rude greeting.

Clara, on the other hand, is gawking. Completely bypassing her sister, she beelines it to me.

"Aiden? God, it's been ages. What brings you here? Were you looking for me?"

Of course she'd think I was here for her. I swallow a groan, not wanting to disrespect Charlotte's sister.

"No, he's not here for you." Charlotte's eyes are ablaze— there's the little spitfire. "He's here for me."

Okay, not exactly how I would've worded it, but it's the truth.

"Excuse me? Last time I checked, you were the senator's *wife*. Is there something you'd like to tell me, sister?" Clara scoffs before returning her gaze to me, her eyes unabashedly roving over my body. *No shame.*

Looking toward Charlotte, I see that she's flustered. Not wanting to leave her hanging, I finally speak up.

"I'm the head of her protective detail. The senator hired us. We're here to ensure your sister's safety." My face remains impassive, although I'd like to tell Clara right where she can shove her righteous attitude. She doesn't have a leg to stand on with how she left things between us, and if she pushes the issue, I'll have to set her straight.

"Oh, that's right. I heard you were the owner of a nationwide security firm. Bravo Aiden." She purses her lips as she continues her perusal, not doing a damn thing to hide what's going through her mind.

"I'm one of five owners."

"Did you come here for something, Clara?" Charlotte is visibly annoyed as she stands in front of me, partially obscuring her sister's view.

I have to chuckle a little. It's adorable how she wants to protect me from Clara's blatant eye fucking.

I guess the chuckle was louder than I thought because she turns around, her big doe eyes glaring.

"Right, I came over to see if you wanted to accompany me to mother's charity luncheon. You always manage to get out of it because of your other engagements. We all know how *important* your life is as the senator's wife. But if you could grace us with your presence, mom would actually get off my back for once."

Clara rolls her eyes as she speaks that last sentence and it takes everything in me not to speak out on behalf of Charlotte.

Who the fuck does she think she is, coming into her sister's home and belittling her time like this.

"I'm sorry. I won't be able to make it. I have a prior engagement with the governor's wife. Maybe next time."

"You've always been a selfish little brat. I should—"

"Enough!" All eyes turn toward me. *Good.* "I'll kindly ask that you reconsider the way you speak to Mrs. Rutherford. We will not tolerate any condescension or abusive behavior toward her. If you have a problem with that, you know where the door is."

Out of the corner of my eye, I can see Titus shaking his head. *I know.* This is definitely breaking protocol. We normally don't interfere with conversations between family members unless they're about to get physical, and we definitely don't talk to a client's family member so informally. But given our history, I figure this merited an exception.

There's no way I would let anyone abuse Charlotte, in any way, shape, or form. She's a light in this dark world—lighting up everything she touches—and I will do everything in my power to keep her that way. Unharmed and untainted.

"I see." Clara's blood-red lips form into a sneer. "Charlotte, I'll be in touch."

Clara whips her hair back and forth as she exits, leaving the air around us lighter and less suffocating with her departure.

"I'm sorry about that." Charlotte's gaze falls to the ground, her cheeks flushing in embarrassment.

Taking her chin between my thumb and forefinger, I lift her face to mine. "There's *nothing* to be sorry about, Charlotte." Our eyes linger longer than appropriate, and it isn't until Titus clears his throat that I'm dropping my hand.

I need to remember to thank him later because just as I do, Senator Rutherford walks in. His eyes land on Charlotte and then me, no doubt noticing our proximity. Narrowing his gaze, he approaches his wife, extending his hand and grabbing a hold of Charlotte's arm. His fingers dig into her soft flesh and I know it will leave a bruise.

My jaw clenches and I'm about to step forward when I feel Titus' hand on my shoulder.

"Aiden, I presume. Michaela gave me your files and they contain *all* of your information." Preston Rutherford extends his free hand in greeting and I begrudgingly accept. After all, he's the one that hired our firm. If I want to keep Charlotte safe, I'll have to play nice with this asshole.

He's the type of pompous prick I'd have expected Clara to end up with, not Charlotte.

"At your service." I give him a tight smile, forcing myself to show some semblance of emotion.

"That's right. At *my* service. Don't forget that." The smug bastard looks toward Charlotte while tightening his already bruising hold.

I'm about to open my mouth to say something when Charlotte shakes her head ever so slightly, her eyes pleading with me not to intervene. *Fuck. I feel so powerless.* S*omething I never allow myself to be.*

"If you'll give us a moment of privacy. I need to speak to *my* wife."

"Of course, Senator." I nod, reluctantly turning around and walking out but not making it farther than the hallway directly outside of the sitting area. After the prick's display of 'power,' you couldn't pay me to stay away. I've seen that look in a man's eyes before, and it never leads to anything good.

Charlotte

"What the fuck was that about, Charlotte?" His voice is low so as not to alert the men in the other room, but loud enough to let me know he won't back down.

"Nothing. Clara was here and she got a little confrontational. Mr. Moretti was just checking to see if I was okay. She brushed by me and I stumbled. That was all." I place a hand on his chest in an attempt to comfort him and feel his breathing slow. Meanwhile, my insides are banging around as I Internalize the disgust at having to touch him.

He's gone during the week for work, and I'm thankful that any physical contact with him is relegated to the weekends.

"Hmm. We can put her on the banned list." My heart begins to soften toward him at the thought that he's actually being protective over me, but then the real motive spills out and I see him for what he truly is. *Selfish.* "We don't want her drawing negative attention toward the family name. We have a reputation to uphold and drama has no place here."

God, if the world really knew what went on inside these four walls. Maybe then I'd be free.

"That won't be necessary. Mr. Moretti made it pretty clear that that type of behavior will not be tolerated."

"At least he's good for something. I swear, Charlotte. I better not catch him touching you, because if I do—"

I wrap my arms around him, catching him off guard and effectively stopping his train of thought. I need to shake him off of Aiden's trail. I love having him here; it brings me comfort in an otherwise hellish world, and if keeping him around means having to placate Preston, then so be it.

"Darling, how was your day? I'm sure it was extremely busy. Everyone wants Senator Rutherford's time." I bat my lashes, hoping he's buying into this charade. Who am I kidding? He loves talking about himself. Of course he's going to take the bait.

Smiling, he squeezes my hips before lifting a hand to brush a loose strand of hair behind my ear and it takes everything in me to not shudder in revulsion.

"Yes, my little doll. They do." He releases me and walks toward the bar area tucked into the far corner, pouring himself a glass of brandy. "But lucky for you, you get to have me at the end of every day."

Well, aren't I a lucky girl.

Chapter Five
CHARLOTTE

C offee. I need coffee.

I got zero sleep last night for fear that Preston would come into the room, demanding I perform my wifely duties. My body shudders at the thought of having to put on an act yet again. *I can't keep living like this.*

I'm beyond grateful that he drank himself to sleep, and I wasn't about to look a gift horse in the mouth by waking him up so I could help him to our room. Thanks to his job, it's been months since we've been intimate. And to be honest, I don't think I could fake it anymore if he'd tried.

If you would've told ten-year-old me that I'd be in a loveless marriage, I would've told you you were crazy. I still believed in true love, fairy tales, and happily ever afters.

But I suppose nothing good ever lasts.

Sandra greets me as she hands me my caffeine fix for the morning, a piping hot cup of coffee with just the right amount of cream and sugar. "Did you sleep well, Mrs. Rutherford?"

I sigh before putting on a smile and nod. "Of course, Sandra. Thank you for asking."

There's no need to tell her the truth. She can't do anything about my current situation, therefore there's no sense in making her worry.

"It's not polite to lie."

Whirling around, I spill my precious coffee in the process. Aiden's rich hazel eyes peer down at me, but his lips hold the whisper of a smirk.

I have no retort. I just stand there, gaping up at him.

Slowly extending his arm, he places his hand under my chin and closes my mouth. "Better keep that closed. Don't want to catch flies, do we?" His eyes narrow, focusing on my mouth, something akin to hunger flashing behind the honey-colored orbs.

Who is this man, and what has he done with stone cold Aiden?

"Excuse me? Do you have the right household? Surely, you can't be my head of security. He's *very* frosty."

Aiden's brow lifts as Sandra snickers behind me. The banter between us is heartwarming, making this cage I'm in bearable.

"If you two will excuse me, I have laundry that needs tending to." Sandra brushes past me as she exits the room, leaving Aiden and me standing there, staring at each other like two awkward teenagers.

"Char-"

"Aid-"

We both move to speak first but end up speaking over one another

"You go first." I give him a bashful smile. I swear this man takes me back to when I was a little girl, pining after her sister's beau.

"Look, I'm not really sure how to broach the subject with someone I'm familiar with."

"Just spit it out."

"Is Preston hurting you?"

The room stands still and all of the air is sucked out of my lungs.

"Charlotte?"

I shake my head no, but no words come out.

"Charlotte..."

"No, Aiden. I mean, he occasionally hurts my feelings if that's what you're asking, then yes." I look out the window, unable to look him in the eyes. Telling him the truth is not an option. Not yet, at least. I need to gather my thoughts and make a plan. Maybe then I'd be able to leave.

If I were being honest, I'd tell him I'm slowly dying inside, becoming a whisper of the woman I once was. Day by day, second by second, he chips away at my soul, robbing me of what little self-worth I have left.

A thumb to my cheek has my gaze flickering back to Aiden. The war raging within his eyes is apparent, and I hate that I'm the cause of it.

"You're crying, Charlotte. Are you sure there isn't anything you want to tell me?" His voice is warm, full of concern and something else I can't quite figure out. *Is it pity?*

Taking a step back, I shake my head once more. Preston is a powerful man, and if I don't play my cards right, I won't be the only one to pay the price. He has the ability to not only destroy me, but those I love. *No.* I need to play his game, making sure I'm the one who comes out on top.

"I'll be in my room. Please don't disturb me unless it's absolutely necessary." Turning on my heels, I practically sprint out of the room.

He's trying to save me, but I'm no damsel and this is no fairy tale.

Aiden

That woman is going to be the death of me. It's obvious she's covering up for someone. The fear in her eyes is palpable, and she's as cautious as a politician on the stand.

Fuck it. If she doesn't want to tell me, then I'll have to dig for the information myself.

Starting with Sandra. She seems to be close to Charlotte. Well, as close as one can get with the walls she puts up.

Finding Sandra in the laundry room, I start on my inquisition.

"Sandra, can I have a moment?"

Clutching her chest, she gasps, "My word. You scared the living daylights out of me, child." She turns to face me, placing her hands on her hips. "Now, what can I help you with?"

"I wanted to talk to you about Charlotte. Know that anything you tell me is in confidence, and if necessary, our team can offer you protection."

With those words, Sandra's face drains of all color and her eyes go as wide as saucers. "I don't know anything."

"Sandra, please. I can't do anything to help her if I don't have concrete proof." My voice is pleading but stern. She needs to understand how serious this is. I have my suspicions that the senator is doing much more than just manhandling her, and going after a man in power is never easy. If we strike, it will have to be with damning evidence.

Chewing on her bottom lip, Sandra nods. "I understand."

"Does that nod mean there is something more going on?"

She opens her mouth to speak but then quickly shuts it, her eyes darting to the door. "Ms. Montgomery, Mrs. Rutherford is in her quarters shall I tell her you're here?"

Turning around I see Clara, a wicked grin spreads across her lips. "Yes, please do."

My jaw clenches in frustration. Right when I was about to get information about Charlotte, Clara intervenes. Ever the pain in my ass. It's a miracle we dated as long as we did. I would've done the honors of splitting us up If she hadn't dropped my ass because of my pedigree.

Don't get me wrong, I was sore about the breakup, but it had nothing to do with losing Clara and everything to do with family pride. I may not be a southern gentleman, but my family name is still a source of pride. Moretti men are conquerors, dominating everything we get our hands on. Fuck anyone who can't appreciate that.

"Now Aiden, is that any way to greet an old lover?" Clara's voice comes out almost a purr, her gleaming eyes raking over my body and stopping short of my crotch.

"We were never lovers, Clara. Or do you not remember? You didn't want to risk tainting your prestigious name with a Moretti bastard."

"Oh, stop. We did plenty of other things, all of which I remember you thoroughly enjoying."

"Everyone should get a pass for doing dumb shit when they're young and naïve. If I would have known then what I know now, I would've steered clear of you, Clarabelle Montgomery."

"You can't still be bitter about our breakup, can you? That was ages ago." She prowls closer, circling me like a predator honing in on its prey. "And my, how deliciously you've changed. Much broader than I remember. Tell me, Aiden. Are you bigger and thicker everywhere?"

A throat clearing has our attention focused back on the door where a very flushed Charlotte glares at her sister. And If looks could kill, Clara would be six feet under.

"Please excuse my sister, she must have forgotten her manners. Coming on to my protective detail is not acceptable and she should know better."

"Come on, Charlotte. Don't be such a prude. It's not like Aiden and I aren't *familiar*."

Something like rage flashes behind Charlotte's eyes, and I can't deny that I enjoy the feeling it stirs inside me.

Come to think of it, Charlotte has always been possessive of me. Even when she was just a girl. She was a major contributing factor as to why I didn't get very far past first base with Clara. Char would somehow interrupt right as things were starting to get steamy.

My eyes narrow as I stare at the beautiful brunette, begging me to wonder if it was all intentional. Her eyes find mine and her whole body flushes an even deeper shade of pink. An image of her naked body turning that gorgeous color beneath me flashes in my mind's eye and I quickly squeeze my eyes shut. *What the fuck.*

"Are you okay, Aiden?" The concern in her voice is genuine, something that's always been there, but I'm only now noticing. "Aiden?"

Opening my eyes, I nod. "Yes. I'm fine. Thank you for worrying about me, but you're the one who needs protecting, not me, little one."

"Honestly, Charlotte. The way you're looking at him, makes me think you still have that childhood crush of yours. Let's not forget, you're a married woman. And besides, we can't have one Montgomery sister go after another's sloppy sec—"

"Enough!" My voice cuts through Clara's tormenting, giving poor Charlotte a break from her sister. "Did you have something you needed to address with the lady of the household, or did you come here to be a nuisance?"

"Aiden, you can't be blind to those big doe eyes, can you?" Clara's lips curl into a sneer and her eyes narrow. "Or have I been a fool and you two have actually had a thing going—"

"Clara!" Charlotte hisses while pointing to the door. "You need to leave. I'm not sure why you're here, but you've done nothing but disrespect me and my staff. Accusing me of things you very well know I wouldn't do is a sure-fire way to get me into trouble."

"Trouble? What has my dear wife done to get into trouble?" Preston walks into the now cramped laundry room and places an arm around Charlotte's shoulder, squeezing her harder than a loving embrace would call for.

My blood boils and my vision darkens. I want to rip his arm off and yell at him for touching her like that. Clenching and unclenching my fists, it takes every shred of self-restraint I possess to keep myself from physically removing her from his grasp.

"Nothing. She's done absolutely nothing wrong. Your visitor, on the other hand," I turn to glare at Clara, "is nothing *but* trouble."

"Aiden, you wound me. I thought we were friends."

Preston's gaze visibly changes from annoyed to amused as his down-turned lips curl into a smirk. "Do you two have a history? How *interesting*." He releases his hold on Charlotte's arm only to wrap his fingers around her bicep. "Come dear, let's leave these two to their lovers' quarrel." Pulling Charlotte by the arm, he moves to exit the room, but before reaching the threshold he turns and sneers, "Charlotte and I will be in my quarters. Do not disturb us under any circumstances. It's been a long day and I've missed *my* wife."

The lilt of his voice as he declared Charlotte his suggests he's not only possessive but jealous. A lethal combination if he's the type of man who gets physical.

Based on his bruising grip, I'd bet my ass he's a fucking coward, taking out his insecurities on those under his control.

"Earth to Aiden. You stare at the door any longer, I'm bound to think you're catatonic."

Breaking from my mental fog, I turn to look at the viper, dressed in refined clothing but dangerous, nonetheless. "Do you realize the chain reaction you've caused for Charlotte? Do you even care that your little stunt is now very possibly costing her a night of peace?"

"What are you talking about? That man adores Charlotte. He buys her anything her little heart desires, and she doesn't have to lift a finger in this palatial home. The girl wants for nothing." Clara rolls her eyes as she flips her hair. Her ignorance of reality is enough to send me through the roof, and I can't hold back. "Not everything is about money, Clara. We do not buy happiness."

"Says the multi-millionaire. Or is it billionaire now that you also own WRATH Securities?" Her lips purse as she begins to look me up and down again, eyeing me as if I were a piece of meat she was about to devour.

"I swear, you ending whatever we had was a blessing. I thank God I was never saddled with your selfish, materialistic ass. Please see yourself out, or I will have one of my men escort you to your car."

The look of sheer indignation on her face would have been enough to make my night. If only I wasn't worried about Charlotte. Leaving Clara behind me, I make my way toward the control room.

It's time I figured out just how physical Preston Rutherford can get.

Chapter Six

AIDEN

"**W**hat the fuck do you mean we don't have access to Preston's bedroom? The *entire* home was wired, as is customary for all of our clients."

Granted, I've never used it to spy, especially when given a direct order from our client to not disturb them. Typically, we use it for surveillance, if—and only if—the client is not in the room or if motion was detected around the perimeter of their quarters.

However, my conscience is perfectly clear when it comes to Charlotte and Preston. I *know* the fucker is up to no good, and I highly doubt he intended on the good kind of physical contact.

The thought of him touching Charlotte in an intimate manner has my lunch threatening to come back up, making me press a hand to my stomach. *What the hell? Since when do I care who Charlotte fucks?*

"You okay, boss? You look sort of green." Jimmy, one of my men, grimaces. "I hate puke. It gives me the skeeves."

I roll my eyes and shake my head, "You're a trained killer, but a little vomit can throw you off your game? Tell me again why I hired you."

"Because I'm one of the best when it comes to tech." He shoots me a proud grin before his statement reminds me of why I'm upset in the first place.

"If you're the best, then why'd you forget to rig up Preston's room?" I cock a brow, waiting for his response.

"I didn't forget, sir. It looks like they were all removed by Mr. Rutherford himself."

My brows knit together as I try to piece together every one of Preston's tells.

He manhandles Charlotte, she's skittish as fuck, and he's secured a dead spot in the home where he can do whatever he wants without eyes on him.

Despite how much I want to pound this man's face into the ground, that's still not enough to justify my doing so.

If he were any other man, I'd march into that room, put him in his place, throw Charlotte over my shoulder and carry her out.

And then what?

Make her mine.

Running my fingers through my hair, I tug at the ends. This is some fucked up shit going on in my head. I dated her sister for fuck's sake. She wouldn't want to be with me.

"Boss? What would you like to do?" Jimmy's voice breaks me out of the mental purgatory I'm in.

Pressing the heels of my palms to my eyes, I groan. "Give me a minute, would you?"

But let's be honest, I'm going to need a whole lot more than a minute to break myself free of whatever the hell is going on inside my head.

Charlotte

My back hits the chair as Preston releases me from his grasp.

"You were standing awfully close to Aiden Moretti the other day and now I walk in on you saying you're getting into trouble," He loosens the knot on his tie as he begins to pace back and forth, "Charlotte, do I need to remind you of who you belong to?"

My body tenses and I turn my face so I'm not directly in his line of vision. I can't let him see the disgust written all over my face.

"Answer me!" Preston roars in my direction, but I still don't turn.

His steps get closer and it's seconds before his cold fingers are gripping my face, physically turning it so I can look into his shit-brown eyes. "I. Asked. You. A. Question." His words come out staccato, as if I'm not mere millimeters away from his mouth, able to hear the vile spewing from his mouth.

"No, Preston. I belong to you. I'm yours and not anyone else's." My tone lacks all emotion, he's drained it all from me, sucking it out of me like the energy vampire that he is.

I know that this will anger him, but I'm too tired to care. Too tired to fight him, too tired to give him what I don't have.

"Don't look so enthused." He snarls before rearing his hand and slapping me with the back of it, the impact leaving a trail of fire across my face. There's no doubt I'll have a welt in a couple of seconds. *Something else to cover up.*

At this point, I'm a walking billboard for camouflage concealers. It hides the darkest of secrets.

Despite the pain I don't cry nor do I say a word. I'm numb. Numb to this shit and as soon as his little show of dominance is done, I'm finding a way out. I can't do this anymore.

One more night of this and I fear I'll lose myself forever. Unable to find my way out of the lies he's fed me.

You are nothing.

You have nothing.

You're just a pretty plaything.

I squeeze my eyes shut, trying to get the words out of my head, but they keep looping over and over again.

"Open your damn eyes, Charlotte. I want you to look at me as I remind you of who you belong to." Preston places his hands on his belt buckle, slowly undoing it and sliding it out of the loops.

My throat constricts and my vision becomes blurry. I can't do this. I can't let him touch me again.

I'm about to stand up and make a run for it when there's a loud bang on the door.

"What part of do not disturb do you not understand!" Preston growls, his temper finally coming through to someone other than myself.

"Senator, it's Governor Howard on the line." Aiden's voice is a beacon of hope. Maybe this hell will be over soon.

Muttering under his breath, Preston refastens his belt and walks toward the door. "This isn't over, Charlotte. I'm coming back as soon as I'm done talking to Howard." Flinging the door open, he glowers at Aiden, attempting to push him as he walks past.

Aiden bites back a smirk, since Preston is unable to move him with his little shove. Well, he's smirking until he takes a look at my face.

Shit. The welt. There's no hiding what just happened. Closing my eyes, I shake my head. A silent plea for him to stay out of it. Preston will be back and I need to find a way to get out without his help. Doing so will only drag him into my mess.

I knew. Deep down I knew marrying him was a mistake, but I wanted to make my father proud. I was never his favorite. Clara always got his love and affection, I was lucky if I ever got a sliver. When Preston started courting me, I suddenly became the favorite daughter. I preened and soaked up every minute of it.

Never in a million years did I think it would come to this.

Tears flow freely down my face and it isn't until a big callused hand is wiping them away that I open my eyes.

Aiden Moretti. My childhood crush stands before me, anger waging a war in those amber eyes. But despite all the rage, his touch is nothing but tender.

This man would never hurt me.

"Char. My *principessa perfetta*. What did he do to you?" This beast of a man is kneeling before me, touching me with gentle affection. So at odds with his usually cold and callous demeanor.

I suck in my lips, unable to respond for fear of unleashing all of the ugly that's been bottled deep inside. I shake my head, hoping he understands that I just can't. I have nothing to give him.

"Charlotte, please. I can't help you if you don't talk to me."

Finding the courage to speak, I finally open myself up a little. "I can't right now. He'll be back any minute."

"No, he won't. The governor promised to keep him on the phone for a while." There's a gleam in his eyes as his words sink in. *My god, did Aiden have governor Howard call Preston on purpose? To distract him? To protect me?*

A slow smile spreads across his luscious lips and I bite my lip, wanting nothing more than to sink my teeth into his instead.

"Don't look at me like that or I'll be forced to do something that we both know isn't right."

"In this world where everything is upside down, who's to say what's wrong and what's right. Can't we make up our own rules?" This brazen outburst surprises the hell out of me. I'm usually the epitome of proper and polite. This is definitely neither.

His eyes narrow before he looks away, and just like that, I've lost him. Retreating into myself, I fall into Preston's words.

You are nothing.

You have nothing.

He's right. What do I have to offer Aiden? I'm broken. A married woman who's coming onto him like an emotionally starved beggar. It's a miracle he hasn't walked out of the room yet.

"Stop." Aiden gently cups my face in the palm of his hands. "I see those wheels turning. We don't need that right now. What we need right now is for you to tell me what that *man* has done to you."

I sigh into his hold, "It'll be my word against his, Aiden. I can't risk it. Nobody will believe me."

He wipes away at a rogue tear, and his affection is my undoing. Tears flow from me, wanting to run away and escape this shell of a body I'm in. If only I could run away with them too.

Aiden's jaw clenches, and I see the reality of our situation in his eyes. He knows it as well as I do, without solid proof we have nothing.

"Don't you worry your pretty little head, my perfect princess." Bringing my face to his, he presses his lips to my forehead, lingering for a few seconds before finally pulling back. "We will get through this together. I give you my word."

I smile despite the tears. A famous Moretti promise is worth its weight in gold.

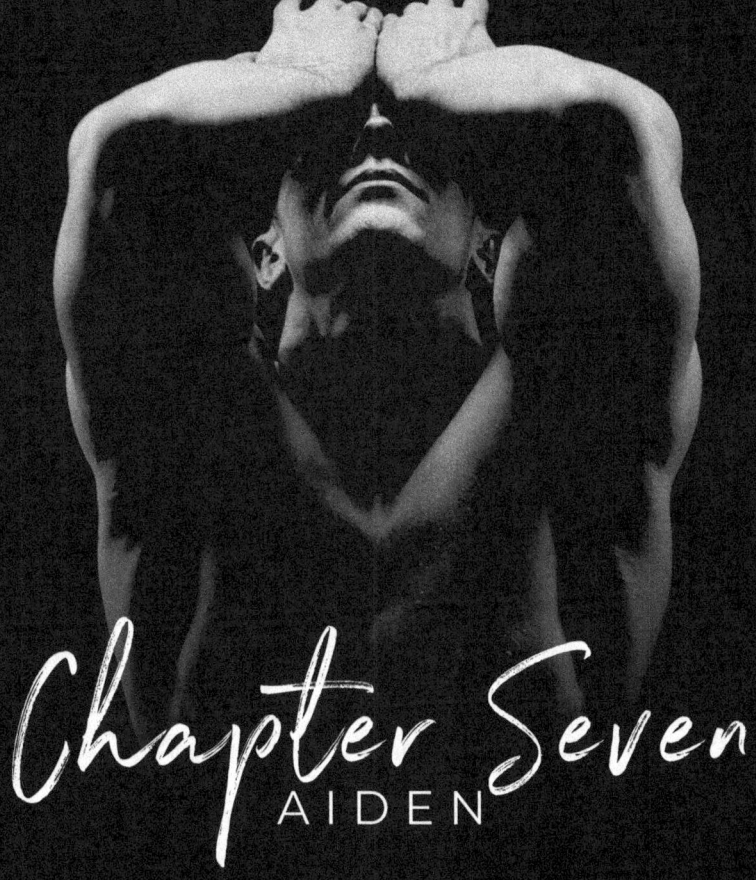

Chapter Seven
AIDEN

"Hold on a sec, let me head into my office." Turning toward the twins, I see their platinum blond hair and piercing blue eyes staring back at me expectantly. We don't have much time together and our weekends are sacred, so the fact that I'm willing to take a work call right now has the boys at full attention.

Weekends are dedicated to my boys. And as much as I love my job, I'll never let it take over my duties as a father ever again. But that doesn't change the fact that Charlotte needs me, and I made a promise to do whatever I could to help her through this situation.

I give the twins a warning as I step away. "I'll be right back. Listen to what Nanny Sylvie tells you and when I come back, I'll join in on the conquest of Black Beard's treasure."

The boys nod in understanding before resuming their imaginary sword fight, forgetting all about my call and remaining blissfully ignorant of the secrets it may hold.

Closing the door to my study, I lift my phone, pressing the button for a video chat as I sit behind my desk. Needing to see their facial expressions as I ask my questions is extremely vital. I'm trained to detect lies and their facial cues can tell me whether they're full of shit or the real deal.

"Marcus, it's been a long time." I smile into the phone, keeping my tone casual.

"Yes, definitely too long. We should remedy that. Beer with the boys soon, yea?"

"Sounds good. I don't normally work on Sundays, but I have a pressing matter that needs addressing."

"Of course, shoot. What's going on?" His eyes show no signs of fear, nothing but genuine concern behind the gray orbs.

"I'm on an assignment for the Rutherford family." His face contorts into one of disgust. Okay, not exactly what I was expecting as his reaction. "It's my understanding that your team was the last to provide a protective detail before we stepped in."

"That's right. And I don't envy your position one bit. Let's just say the senator is a special case and working for him has been my *least* favorite job. *Ever.*"

That's very telling. The man has been in actual combat with enemy insurgents who aren't shy about torture and whose tactics in battle are anything but fair.

I run my hand over my face, "You know I'm going to need more than that, friend. I suspect you know how the senator treats his wife and what he's accused you of."

Marcus scoffs into the phone, "Between you and me, that sick bastard is possessive of his wife beyond all reason. His obsession with her has twisted into his dark corrupt soul and made him see things that aren't there."

His words have me releasing a breath I didn't know I was holding. "So you *never* touched her in an unprofessional manner?" I know it's pushing, but I need him to thoroughly spell it out for me.

A look of pain flashes across his face as if my words have physically wounded him, "Brother, I thought you would know me better than that. I would never be so unprofessional on a job, and I most definitely would never even entertain the thought of being intimate with a married woman."

It's my turn to be wounded. Though his words aren't intended to do so, they remind me of the illicit thoughts running wild in my head. Despite how much I try to shove them out, visions of a very naked and very flushed Charlotte writhing beneath me are all I can see.

"Right. I know, but I had to ask because..."

Marcus' eyes narrow. "What? Is the bastard accusing one of your men of having intimate relations with his wife too? That's rich. Your men would never do that. Your reputation isn't what it is for nothing."

His blind faith in my team fills me with a source of pride, although if he knew the thoughts running through my head, I'm pretty sure he'd feel differently.

"That's right. Our team would never step out of line like that. But I was more concerned with how he physically treats her. Did you notice anything alarming when you were in charge?"

His whole upper body stiffens and a look of discomfort flashes across his face. "To be honest, we did notice that he was very handsy with her, and not in a fun way. His grip was almost bruising in our presence, but it was never more than that." His jaw clenches and his eyes glaze over. "Had it been, we definitely would have intervened. Have things progressed beyond a firm hold?"

Not wanting to give too much away, I school my features. "There's concern, but we lack sufficient evidence to be able to do anything about it. As you know, taking down a man of his social stature requires a little more finesse than our typical Joe. Not saying that it can't be done, we just need to be smart about it."

Marcus nods in agreement. "Have the surveillance cameras caught anything or the staff come forward with corroborating statements?"

"No to either. The man is smart, going so far as to create a dead spot in his home where he can do anything without eyes. And the fear he's instilled in his staff... well, I'm sure you noticed."

"Yes, we did. Although the cook looks like she has a soft spot for Charlotte. She might be of some assistance." He offers me a half-hearted smile, knowing that it would be extremely unlikely for someone to openly wrong the senator.

"Right. I tried talking to her but was stopped by a ghost from my past."

Marcus raises a brow, a smirk playing across his thin lips. "Is there something I'm missing?"

"A tale for another time. Maybe over drinks. Lots and lots of drinks."

We both chuckle before I thank him for his help and once again agreeing to a night out soon.

Well, that was enlightening.

I quickly shoot Titus a message informing him of what I've just learned. He's currently at the Rutherford residence, making sure the senator is keeping his hands to himself.

Running my hands through my hair, I tilt my head back in supplication. For what, I don't know.

Peace? Patience? Understanding?

Even though Marcus confirmed that nothing went on between himself and Charlotte, I can't help but feel tied up inside about her being a possible cheater. No, she didn't do anything with Marcus or his men, but she was more than willing to kiss me last night.

That must mean something, right?

But then again, I'm vehemently against cheaters and there I was, almost willing to break my own damn rules just for a taste of those lips... Those deliciously juicy and forbidden lips which I've pictured wrapped around my throbbing cock on multiple occasions.

Fuuuuuuck. I'm in deep.

Palming my stiffening erection, I mentally slap myself. If I don't watch myself, I'm bound to become the very thing I hate, and that's not something I'm willing to accept.

Chapter Eight
CHARLOTTE

He's not here and I feel the loss like a brick to the chest. It's Aiden's day off and I'm missing him something fierce. I know a married woman isn't supposed to feel this way toward another man, but there should be an exception for Aiden. My childhood crush and my accomplice, helping me escape my living nightmare.

Titus is here today, and no offense to him, but I just don't feel as safe without Aiden. Like a blanket of safety, enveloping me in its warmth—Aiden always comes through. Always has, and I suspect he always will.

I'm at my vanity, getting ready for the day when a dark shadow eclipses me. My body stiffens, sensing the monster that lurks behind me.

"Who are you getting all dolled up for? It's Sunday and we don't have any engagements today." Prestons voice is cold, lacking any emotion, sending chills up my spine and my stomach tightening in anticipation. *What will his next move be?*

Looking into the mirror, I see his facial expression matches his tone.

"Nobody, Preston. I'm just getting ready with minimal makeup. You know I always get ready for the day, even if it's just tinted moisturizer with a high SPF. Gotta combat skin cancer, right?" I give him my best attempt at a warm smile, but it does nothing to change his sour mood.

"Liar. You're just a fucking liar. That's all that comes out of your mouth." Finally, some emotion. Unfortunately, it's not a happy one.

"Can we *not* do this today? I just want a peaceful morning. Please." I close my eyes and suck in a deep breath. "Agh!" I yelp as Preston digs his fingers into my hair, yanking back forcefully.

"*Do not* give me sass, Charlotte. I am not in the mood."

"I noticed." I mumble, knowing this will only set him off further, but I just don't give a shit anymore.

As expected, he doesn't take kindly to my talking back. My shoulder is the first to hit the floor, followed by the rest of my body.

I quickly scurry away from him, making sure to never give him my back. Once I've gained enough distance, I stand and hold my ground. "Enough. Enough of you pushing me around and talking down to me, Preston. I will not tolerate it. You want to have this farce of a marriage, fine. I can play your game so that you can save face. But I will not allow you to keep treating me like garbage."

Preston's face is the depiction of shock. He never thought his precious little Charlotte would ever have the balls to talk back to him, but surprise-surprise, even I have a breaking point.

"If you don't want to be treated like garbage, then don't act like garbage."

I close my eyes and shake my head in frustration. No matter what I tell him, he will always find a way to twist things in his favor.

"Look, think what you want, but I'm not going to be a part of it." Grabbing my bag off of the night stand, I head toward the door. "I'm heading to my sisters. See you—"

His cold hand grabs at my hair, pulling me back toward him and slamming me against his chest. I can feel his breathing down my neck, my body reacting to his and freezing up as a form of self-preservation. "You aren't going anywhere, my little doll. I'm not done with you."

"If you don't let me go right now, I'm going to scream so loud people three blocks down will hear. And we don't want that, do we?"

"Fucking bitch." Preston slams me against the door, ripping the bag from my hands in the process. "If you want to leave, then you'll have to do it without this." He waves my purse in the air like a maniac before throwing it against the opposite wall, his face contorting into a sneer. "I've given you everything. You are nothing without me. Everything you are, everything you own, it's all because of me. So if you want to leave right now, then you'll have to do it without clothes." He rips at my blouse while his spittle lands on my face. "Your family doesn't even want you. Your father couldn't wait to hand you over to me. You think you get to call the shots now because you've suddenly grown a pair? Think again, Charlotte."

My body gives up the fight and I fall limp in his grasp. His words have hit their intended target, my heart. It shatters and the silent tears start flowing freely down my face. *I'm nobody. Nobody wants me.*

Pounding on the door breaks me from my self-pity, throwing me into action. I grab at a dressing gown hanging behind the door and throw it on, hiding the torn silk underneath.

"Sir, Ma'am. There's a disturbance in this wing and we'd like you to vacate into the safe room with our team." Titus' voice booms through the door, his sense of authority bringing me some sense of calm.

Aiden

"Why the fuck are they in the safe room? I didn't get any alerts notifying me of any disturbances on the property." My brows come together as I look at Titus, waiting for an explanation. I was pulled away from my Sunday with the boys because of this emergency, yet I'm betting it has nothing to do with an exterior threat and everything to do with my *principessa perfetta* and her husband.

He huffs out in frustration. "It's the only thing I could think of doing to stop the yelling match that was going on behind their closed doors." He runs a hand through his hair and this is no doubt stressful for the man who doesn't deal with emotions well—or at all, really. "Look, it was either put them in the safe room or let them go at each other until he did god knows what to Charlotte."

My whole body bristles at this news. "What the fuck happened, and so help me God, you better give me every damn detail because I should've been called as soon as this shit developed."

Titus cocks a brow but doesn't comment on my outburst of emotion. "We performed a sweep of the home earlier today and found these." He hands me a small recording device before continuing. "We were going to install the cameras in the master bedroom, but when we saw that we were being recorded, no doubt by Mr. Rutherford himself, we decided it would be best to just finish the sweep and bring up our findings with Preston upon finishing. The last thing we wanted to do was alert him to the fact that we're on to him."

I nod in complete agreement. "Okay, I get not wanting to show our cards, but what does that have to do with what transpired with Charlotte?"

"Right when we finished our sweep, Preston requested we vacate the left wing, claiming that he wanted some time with his wife. We tried to bring up the devices we found during our sweep but he downplayed it, saying he would discuss it after his 'family time.' The best we could do is keep our ears on the area since we didn't have eyes." His lips purse to the side while he shakes his head. "I feel fucking terrible for Charlotte. You should have seen her when he finally opened the door. Thankfully, there were no signs of physical abuse, but her hair was a mess and her eyes were glossy, as if she'd just been crying."

"*Shit.* We need to do something, Titus. This can't continue." I rub my forehead, knowing we need to come up with a plan right-the-fuck-now. "I spoke with Marcus earlier today and he confirmed having the same suspicions but that he never really saw anything that would, in his eyes, warrant further interference on their part."

Titus smirks, "Well, it's not like he has a personal interest in Charlotte like you do."

"Careful," I warn, my tone leaving no room for interpretation. I will not tolerate insinuations of that nature. Not only will it smear Charlotte's name, but I under no circumstances will be at fault for causing someone to be unfaithful to their partner—regardless of how fucked up their marriage is.

Titus bites back a smile but adds no further comment. "So, what's the plan, Hoss. You know I've got your back. I'll follow your lead."

"While they're in the panic room, we go ahead and add eyes and ears to the dead zones. Then we let them out and catch him in the act. We then barge in and tell him to release her from his grasp, both physically and metaphorically, and we get Charlotte the hell out of here."

Titus nods, "Very well. I'll round the men and we'll get right on it."

I sigh a breath of relief. Soon this shit show will be over and Charlotte will be safe.

Will she, though?

Like the warrior she is, her scars will remain with her long after she's left.

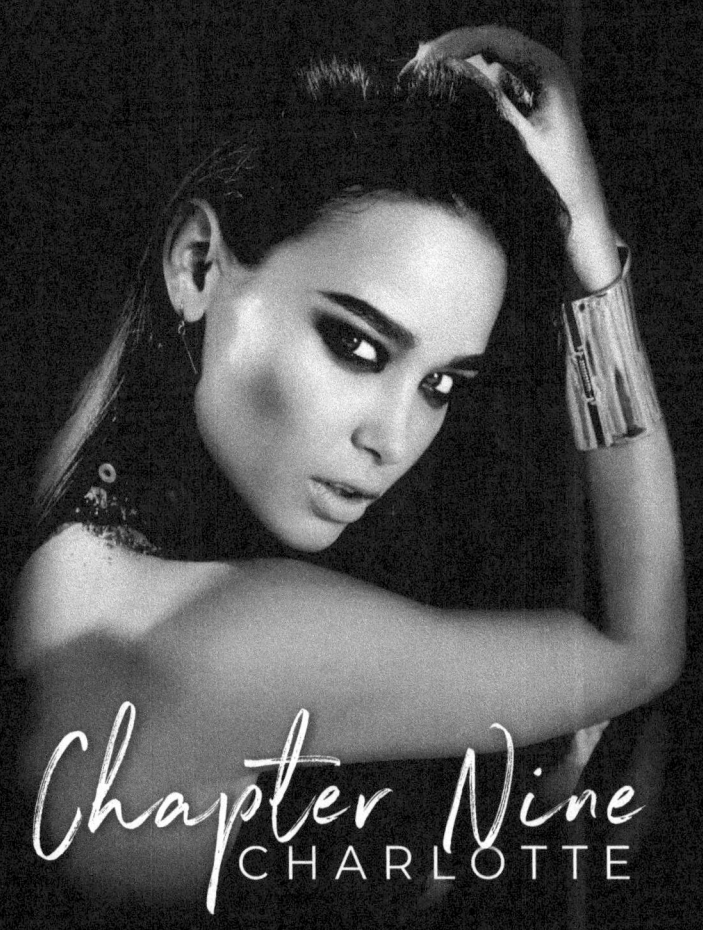

Chapter Nine
CHARLOTTE

*T*alk about awkward. Preston and I are stuck in a room the size of a large walk-in closet with two other men. There's nowhere to escape his penetrating stare.

He's looking at me as if it's my fault we're in this predicament. *Please.* I roll my eyes, not caring that it will only infuriate him further. What's he going to do? Hit me in front of my protective detail?

"How much longer are we going to be in here?" Preston growls at one of the men, his nostrils flaring and mouth puckering in obvious displeasure.

"Sir, we have to wait until we've received an all-clear. Until then, it's in your best interest to remain in this room."

"What's the matter, Preston, aren't you enjoying the company?" I give him my sweetest smile, knowing he can't fault me for playing the role of a loving wife in front of others. I'm the only one who knows how deeply that comment burrows under his skin.

He accuses me of not having the love of my family, yet he's the one who's emotionally bankrupt—needing to control everyone around him, forcing them into the farce of adoration.

"My sweet Charlotte, I could never tire of your beautiful face." His eyes narrow and his lips begin to lift ever so slightly at the corners. *Shit.* I know that look.

I've gone and poked the bear, and he is never one to take things lying down. I only pray that I can find my way out of whatever he's scheming.

Daniel, the taller of the two men, presses his hand to his ear. No doubt listening to whatever is being radioed to him by Titus.

"Looks like we've just received the okay to open the door."

Preston shoves past Daniel, mumbling under his breath, "Let me guess, they found nothing." Stopping at the door, he turns and his ice-cold eyes clash with mine. "Charlotte, come with me. I have a surprise for you."

I practically stumble forward. *This is not good.*

"Sure, just need to talk to Sandra first. She had my silk blouse steamed." I wave my hand over the satin dressing gown I'd thrown on when Titus knocked on our door. "I can't very well wear this all day, now can I?"

"Be quick about it. I promise, you'll want to hear about your surprise as soon as possible." A slight raise of his brows lets me know that this surprise will not be an enjoyable one.

"Right. Of course." With a quick nod, I'm off and heading in the opposite direction of my bedroom.

I'm about to walk past the laundry room in search of Sandra when a hand reaches out, grabbing my hand and pulling me from the hallway.

I'm met with a pair of amber eyes, glistening with concern. "*Charlotte.*" Aiden's left hand anchors me, holding on tightly to my own, while his right hand caresses my face. "Are you okay?"

"Yes, but I think Preston is planning something. I'm not sure what, but things got pretty intense earlier and then, in the panic room..." I look away, not really wanting to voice what's running through my mind.

"Talk to me, *principessa.*" His voice is barely a whisper, but that term of endearment is enough to make my whole body erupt in goose bumps.

Closing my eyes, I take in a deep breath before answering. "The look in his eyes, Aiden. I think he knows I've had enough and if he can't have his way, then... I'm not sure how far he's willing to take it."

Silence lingers between us as we both ponder whether Preston is capable of offing his dear little wife now that she's not playing by his rules.

"Well, we just won't let it get that far." Aiden squeezes my hand before continuing. "We've set up eyes and ears in all of the dead zones. There's no way we won't catch him red handed. As soon as we have what we need, we'll get you out." Placing his hand under my chin, he tilts my face upward. "We will get you out, Charlotte. You just need to hang in there."

My lips roll in and away from Aiden. If we stand like this much longer, I'm not sure I'd be able to keep them away from him.

My whole body comes alive when I'm around him. It's as if he's the sun and I'm a thirsty flower trying to catch his rays.

Sensing the tension between us, he releases his hold on me and steps back. Clearing his throat, he extends his hand toward the door. "Better get going, don't want to give Preston more ammo than necessary." His lips form into a thin line as if it pains him to say the words.

"Right. Okay then." I walk past him and toward a brighter future. Unfortunately for me, I'll have to trudge through a river of darkness before I come out on the other side.

Aiden

Stepping away from her is getting harder and harder. I need to keep physical distance from her from now on.

Placing a hand on my shoulder, Titus squeezes. "You okay, brother?"

It's no secret I don't really do emotion, especially after my injury, but admitting what's really going through my head right now is something entirely different. I'm not even willing to voice it in my own head, let alone fess up my fucked up feelings to one of my best friends.

"Yeah, as right as rain. What are you still doing here? You know I've got this." I give him a salacious grin. "But if you want to stick around for this bust, I don't mind."

Titus chuckles, "You know me well. There's no way I'd pass up on bagging a scumbag with his level of influence. What's that saying? The bigger they are, the harder they fall."

"Something like that."

Soft chatter in the bedroom has me zeroing in on their conversation.

"Preston, what are you talking about? I have prior engagements. I can't just drop everything and go yachting with you." Charlotte's voice sounds panicked, and rightfully so. Seems like he has sprung a trip on her.

"What's more important than a little bonding time with your husband? I'd say hanging out on our yacht, enjoying some quality time is a hell of a lot better than being here all day." I zoom in on the visuals and see that his eyes are narrowed and his face is menacing, despite the sweet undertone of his voice. "Unless there's another reason you'd like to stay home... is there something you want to tell me, Charlotte? Have you been opening those whore legs of yours to the staff again? Is that why you'd rather stay here than take a short trip with your husband?"

"Preston, stop. Stop accusing me of shit you very well know I haven't done." Charlotte slowly steps away from the bastard, no doubt sensing he's about to pounce on her. "I've given my word, that's all. You don't want me to break my word to the governor's wife, do you?" She puts on an encouraging smile, but the warmth doesn't quite reach her eyes. "I say we just reschedule for later in the month. It will be nicer weather anyway."

"Ah, ah, ahh." Preston waves his finger back and forth as if admonishing a child. "Where do you think you're going, my dear wife? Don't think I don't notice you inching your whorish legs toward the door." With two quick strides, he's reached Charlotte, grabbing hold of her arms and shaking her once. "Have you forgotten, dear? You're mine. Mine to play with, mine to dress, and only mine to fuck."

Holding myself back from bursting into the room prematurely, I clench and unclench my fists, needing to call on every ounce of willpower I possess. Apparently, Titus sees right through me because he has both hands on either side of my head, pressing down on my shoulders and keeping me in place.

Charlotte flinches as Preston grabs a hold of her hair, wrapping it around his fist. "How could I forget? You remind me of it every fucking day."

I go to leave, but Titus holds me back. "We need more, brother. This isn't enough to really bury him."

I squeeze my eyes shut for a second, tilting my head back in frustration. I know he's right. If we want to make this stick, then we need a little more. "We definitely need to get to them before they leave. I do not want them alone on that boat together. Something tells me Preston wouldn't be keen on having our team on board."

Titus cringes. "Yea, it's all a little too *suspicious* if you ask me. Like he's planning on 'handling' her on the boat, where no one will see."

My lips press into a thin line. I'd been thinking the same thing but wasn't ready to voice it out loud.

"If he had those bugs of his planted before his last tussle with Charlotte, then it's possible he overheard my conversation with her. And if that's the case, he knows his days are numbered. Unfortunately, we both know that a cornered man is an unpredictable one. I can't risk him being with her a moment longer than necessary."

Looking at the closed circuit TV, I mentally will Charlotte to react. *Come on, baby. Push that bastard's buttons.*

My stomach churns, either from the tension transpiring in the other room or at the fact that I've just called a married woman *baby.* Unwilling to entertain the internal debate any further, I begin to walk toward their wing of the home. Pointing at the piece in my ear, I turn to Titus "Tell me when it's time. I want to be right outside their door, swooping in for the kill."

Titus nods, shooting me a wicked grin. I swear, we all live for the action, but Titus takes a special pleasure in it. If I didn't know any better, I'd even say it was his driving source.

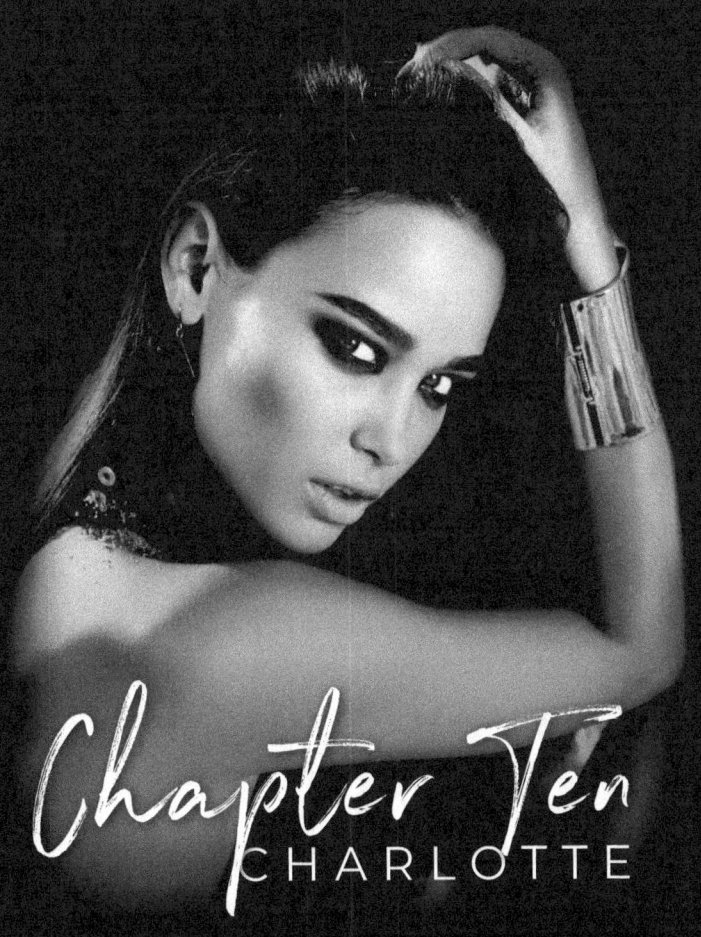

Chapter Ten
CHARLOTTE

My body erupts into chills, goose bumps covering every inch of my body. I've never seen him this detached before. It's as if he isn't even in there, nothing but hatred driving his actions.

"Preston, stop. You're scaring me." My voice comes out barely a whisper, but it's all I can muster. Evil is the only way I could describe him right now. It's as if I were staring right at the devil himself.

A sneer dances across his lips. "Why? Am I scaring you? Are you hiding something? Want to tell me something about you and *Aiden?*"

Shit, shit, shiiiiit.

He knows. He fucking knows. *But how?* I haven't acted out on any of my feelings. The closest I've come to it was the other day when Aiden interrupted with the governor's calls. *God.* Did he somehow overhear our conversation?

My body begins to shake. That's it. This is it. There's no doubt in my mind that this little trip of his is his idea of disposing of me.

Putting on my mask of indifference, though my body betrays me, I pull one last ditch effort at securing my safety. "Of course not, Preston. If you insist on going through with this little getaway, then I suggest we bring our detail with us. Especially with the perceived threat we just had. One can never be too safe, right?" I press my lips together and smile, fighting back the tears of terror that are threatening their way out.

"You'd like that wouldn't you." Preston releases me from his hold only to pace directly in front of me. "No, Charlotte. This trip is just for you and I. A reward for all that you've *done.*"

My body deflates back against the wall. It's now or never, Charlotte. Either bring out his monster here in front of the cameras or face it out on the open sea where none will be the wiser as he throws me overboard, quite literally feeding me to the sharks.

"No." My head held high, I stare into his soulless pits of disdain.

"No, what?" Preston cocks a brow as if sensing my little game.

"To be quite honest, I don't feel safe. If you won't agree to having our detail on board, then I'm not going."

"But Charlotte, we don't need them. The only people on board will be you and me, your husband."

"Precisely. With your track record, I'm not looking forward to being in close quarters with your Hyde."

His eyes narrow as he lunges for me, grabbing both of my hands and pinning them above me. "I haven't got the slightest clue as to what you're referring to, my dear."

"This. This is what I'm talking about. Your voice is as sweet as honey, but your bruising grip on my wrists is crushing. It hurts. Let me go."

"Are you scared?" A cackle falls from his lips and I see the monster threatening to peek through.

"Of a coward like you? Never. You've wrongfully accused me of being with multiple men by this point. Calling them worthless and garbage. Well, I'm here to tell you that ten of you would never amount to one of them. You are a horrible husband and at this very moment I wish that all of your accusations were true." Closing my eyes, I tell him my truth. "Maybe then I'd be free of you. Free of this cage you've trapped me in."

"You ungrateful bitch!" Preston flings me to the floor, my body landing at his feet. "After everything I've done for you, everything I've given you. You were *nothing before me.* You will be *nothing* after me."

Crouching down to my level, his hand reaches up to my throat, effortlessly crushing my windpipe while his knee lands on my sternum—keeping me from getting up.

My arms flail, trying to grasp at his arm and prying it from my neck, but I'm not as strong as he is. "Sssssssst." I try telling him to stop—warn him that he's killing me—but all that comes out is a strangled hiss.

As everything begins to fade, I hear a loud crashing sound. Suddenly Preston is being lifted from my body as he goes flying across the room.

Aiden.

I'm not one to believe in a knight in shining armor, but right this very second, looking at Aiden in all of his six-foot-three glory, no other title would fit. He charges toward Preston, his toned and chiseled body looming over the man crumpled on the floor.

"Get up! Get up, you *fucking* coward! I refuse to hit you while you're lying on the ground."

"Security!" The bastard has the balls to yell out for *my* protective detail, as if they don't know what he's been doing to me behind closed doors.

"Cry all you want, little man, they aren't coming for you." Lifting Preston by his shirt, Aiden helps him to standing. "You might have fooled many, playing the part of a loving husband. But we both know that when you're behind these four walls, you're nothing but a coward, taking out your insecurities on a woman that is far too good for you."

"You don't know what you're talking about. You're just some muscle head that nobody will believe. It's your measly word versus that of their senator." Preston has the balls to chuckle while his body dangles in the air from Aiden's hold. *Unbelievable.*

"Yes. They'll have my word, but they'll also have the footage and audio to corroborate the very thorough statement I plan on giving." A full toothy grin spreads across Aiden's lips and my breath catches. God, that man is gorgeous, but when he smiles he quite literally takes my breath away.

Preston's face turns the color of a tomato and I can't help but cackle. It's a full blown maniacal laugh, emerging from all of the repressed anger and sadness I've carried over the years. Tears fall down my cheeks as I bowl over, clutching my stomach as my chest rises and falls with each laugh.

"You fucking who—" Preston's face whips back as Aiden's fist slams into his nose, blood quickly trickling down Preston's face.

My hands fly to my mouth as I suck in air. I don't know what I was expecting, but it definitely wasn't Preston getting clocked out.

"You'll pay for that, prick." Preston gargles as the blood trickles down his lips and onto his perfectly pressed dress shirt—the blood red a stark contrast to the bright white. "If you come after me, I'll be sure to make the rest of your life a living hell. You think you can leave this house with your so-called evidence? Please. I'll have the police here before you can say Miranda rights."

"You're bluffing and we both know it. Besides, everything that's been recorded in this room is sent to our server. Our server which is saved to the cloud. The cloud which can be accessed anywhere in the world, as long as you have access to Wi-Fi." Aiden backs away from Preston, extending his hand toward me and helping me off of the floor. "If you value whatever dignity you have left, you will let us leave with Charlotte—peacefully."

Chewing on my lip nervously, we pause a few feet from the door, waiting on Preston's response. The ideal situation would be for him to admit defeat and just let me leave. He can keep the clothes, the car, the damn house. I don't need a damn thing if he'd just let me go.

"Charlotte is *miiiiiiine!*" Preston charges toward Aiden, flinging his entire body forward, arms outstretched and hands reaching.

Unfortunately for him, Aiden is a SEAL. With one swift movement, Aiden releases my hand, spins counterclockwise, stopping directly behind Preston and securing him in a choke hold.

"Titus, please remove Charlotte while I deal with the *senator*." His eyes find mine, and despite the murderous rage that's dancing around the irises, I feel his warmth, silently reassuring me that everything is going to be okay.

With a nod, I feel Titus' hand gently tapping my shoulder. I was so entranced in Aiden's gaze that I totally missed him entering the room.

"Ms. Montgomery, will you please come with me?"

Blinking my eyes a few times, I finally nod. "Yes, of course."

Following Titus out of the room, I look back once more and see that Aiden's arm is still firmly wrapped around Preston's neck as he begins to walk my husband's body toward a chair, his legs violently kicking in a futile effort to get away.

My face scrunches up at the sight before me.

Not at the idea of what Aiden will do to Preston, but at the idea that it actually brings me some twisted sense of satisfaction.

Chapter Eleven
AIDEN

After getting cleaned up at the office, I head to the safe house. It's not fancy by any stretch of the imagination. Just a simple home on the outskirts of DFW. No one would suspect that the light blue home with white shutters and wraparound porch has housed the Renzetti Famiglia and now the senator's wife seeking refuge.

The *senator's* wife. I need to remind myself of that before stepping through that doorway. If I thought Charlotte was tempting before, being in close quarters with just the two of us is going to be excruciating torture.

I enter the small living area and her scent of amber and lilac hits my nose, unexpectedly making my cock twitch. *Yup. I'm fucked.*

"Aiden?" Charlotte's flustered face peeks from around the staircase, Titus following close behind. "Thank god!" She rushes toward me, wrapping her thin arms around my waist.

Like a deer in headlights, I stare at Titus who just offers me a smirk and shrug of the shoulders. Not knowing what to do with my arms awkwardly hanging on either side of me, I wrap them around her tiny frame, and all at once my chest constricts, my heartbeat picks up, and my breathing intensifies.

Unable to help it, my nose follows the curve of her jaw, landing on the crook of her neck and inhaling deeply.

How can something so wrong feel so right?

Someone clearing their throat behind me has me stirring from my thoughts, and then I remember we aren't alone. Turning to look at Titus, I see he's still wearing that fucking smirk.

"I'll leave you guys to it. A couple of our guys are stationed outside and in the house catty-cornered to this one. Just radio if you need anything. And I do mean *anything*." His lips purse, pleased with his own brand of humor.

Glaring, I flip him the finger. "Thanks for your help, brother. We'll talk about the details tomorrow. For now, go rest. You've been on for over forty-eight hours."

"Ten-four." And with a salute, Titus closes the door behind him.

It's so quiet you could hear a pin drop. Finally turning back toward Charlotte, I see that her face is pink, and she's completely avoiding my gaze. Taking my thumb and forefinger to her chin, I lift her face toward mine and look deep into her chocolate eyes. *She's so damn beautiful.*

"You going shy on me, *principessa?*" The corners of my mouth lift into a gentle smile in an attempt to reassure both of us.

This is uncharted territory for me, and based on what I've uncovered, I'm pretty sure it is for her as well.

"I can't help it. Being around you has a way of turning me into this awkward teenage version of myself." Her eyes sparkle and I see the awe behind them.

My thumb gently begins to stroke her cheek back and forth as my gaze falls to her lips. She bites her plump lower lip and I immediately drop my hand as if it's touched a scorching hot iron.

She's still married, and if I let myself taste her now, I'll be no better than my late wife.

Unfortunately, my quick withdrawal has her face falling. Needing to remedy the situation, I try to make sense of my actions. "Charlotte, you know we can't do anything. You're still married. And if I keep touching you like I just did... Well, let's just say it wouldn't be long before I had you pinned against that wall, panting my name."

Charlotte's mouth is hanging open as her eyes blink rapidly. "Aiden Moretti, you cannot say something like that to me and not expect a damn response."

I bite back a grin, knowing full well that I've given her a visual that's probably left her panties soaked. Choosing to change the subject before things get too hot, I bring up the reality of our situation. "So, the next move is up to you, Char. What do you want to do now that you are on your way to freedom from that bastard?"

Looking me up and down, I see the wheels turning, but I know she won't voice whatever it is she's thinking out loud. Pursing her lips to the side, she finally answers while strolling to the small loveseat.

"Sit with me and I'll tell you."

My brow lifts as I playfully give her the side-eye. There's plenty of seating in this living room, but denying Charlotte is not something I like doing. Sitting next to her, I turn so that I'm fully facing her, our knees butting up against one another. "Okay, I'm sitting. Spill it."

Her soft giggle has my cock coming alive in my slacks. Resting my arms on my knees, I'm able to hide my body's reaction to her.

"First, I want to say thank you. I couldn't have done this on my own."

"Stop." I lift a hand, telling her to go no further. "You are one of the strongest women I know, Charlotte. Do not belittle your strength. You definitely would have found a way to get out of that toxic relationship. Don't think I didn't notice that go-bag of yours. You've been ready to fly for a while now. Just needed the right moment to do it and I'm glad I was able to be a part of that for you."

A lone tear falls down her cheek and my hand reaches to wipe it away. Apparently I'm unable to keep myself from touching her.

"Thank you. I mean it, Aiden. For helping me escape and now piecing my self-confidence back together." She tucks a loose strand of her hair behind her ear before looking away. "So, I was thinking I would talk to an attorney tomorrow. I want to file for divorce but I'm not sure how to go about it since it will no doubt be such a high profile matter and I'm not exactly looking forward to ending up in the news. That is, if Preston hasn't declared his wife kidnapped already." She nibbles on her lip, looking at me for answers.

"He won't be bothering you again, *principessa*. Of that you can be sure." No trace of humor is left on my face. My eyes narrow and I hold her gaze until I see the flicker of understanding behind her own. "Our in-house counsel can point us toward the right family law attorney. He doesn't typically handle that type of case, but he has some really good connections and will help you find the right fit."

"Okay, then." Charlotte licks her lips while rubbing the palms of her hands on her thighs, practically tasting full-fledged freedom. "So what do we do until then?"

I feel my face heat. Not being one who typically blushes, I'm pretty sure she knows what's going through my head.

Clearing my throat, I fill her in on her new detail schedule. "I'll be staying here with you until the divorce is final. Being the head of your detail, I don't feel right leaving you here with anyone else. Especially since we don't know how the public will react to the change in your relationship status."

"But what about your boys? Won't they miss you?" Her face turns pink and her gaze falls.

"So you know about my twins?" The corner of my mouth lifts. It's good to know she's been keeping tabs on me all this time.

Through thick lashes, Charlotte looks up and slowly nods. "Yes, and I'm so sorry for your loss. I wanted to send my condolences three years ago, but I didn't think it was my place since we hadn't spoken in ages."

Like an unexpected storm rolling in, my whole body goes from feeling warm to frigid in ten seconds flat. Memories of my cheating wife are not something I'd like to entertain right now. "About the boys, if it's okay with you, I was planning on bringing them here along with their nanny, Sylvie. You're used to Sandra, so she'd be able to help with anything you need and this way, I won't have to alienate the twins while still being on the job."

Charlotte brings her hands to her face, groaning into her palms. "Ugh, I don't want to put the boys in danger by being here with me. I mean, I'd love to meet them but if it's going to be too dangerous for them, then maybe you should go home and have Titus take your place here."

The fact that this woman is willing to put my boys before her own desires is proof enough for me that she has a heart of gold. Preston was a damn fool to mistreat her. "It's very sweet of you to worry, but we are safe here. We've got more security outside and Preston would be long intercepted before stepping a foot on that wraparound porch." Pointing toward the door, I give her a reassuring smile. "So what do you say... are you in?"

"I'm in." Her eyes meet mine as her hands reach for me, her fingertips caressing the sensitive skin of my forearms and sending a shiver of pleasure running through me.

As if being pulled by a magnet, my body moves closer to hers, unable to keep myself from touching her in return. My hands gravitate toward either side of her hips, digging my fingers into her soft flesh, my lips hovering above hers. The tip of Charlotte's tongue hesitantly reaches out, brushing my lower lip, and making me groan into her mouth. *Fuuuuuck.* If a simple lick feels this good, I can only imagine what that wicked little mouth will feel like wrapped around my cock.

Squeezing my eyes shut, I give myself a mental slap. She's still a married woman, and this shit right here is playing with fire. This past year has been a compilation of poor decisions on my part, ultimately affecting those I love. *No more.*

"Char—we can't do this." Pulling my hands back, I see her face fall and it breaks my heart into a million little pieces. Lifting her face to mine, I look deep into her mocha eyes, needing to show her how much she means to me. "You know I'm doing this for you, right? I don't want your name to be tarnished. I respect you too much for that."

Her lips press into a thin line as she slowly nods, a flush beginning to creep up her neck and face. "Yeah, you're right. I'm sorry."

"There's no need to apologize, *principessa*. This was as much my doing as it was yours." Biting on my lower lip, I try to keep myself from reliving the sensation of her tongue on my mouth. "I just need to learn to keep my hands to myself."

This earns me a soft smile, Charlotte's face lighting up with a lightness I haven't seen on her in decades. "Is that a challenge I hear?"

"Oh no, little one. There will be no challenge. It's already too damn tempting and you trying to sabotage my attempts at safeguarding your virtue will not be fair."

"Haven't you heard?" Charlotte gets up from the loveseat, cocking a brow as she begins to walk away, hips in full swing. "All is fair in love and war."

Damn. Falling onto the backrest, my heart lurches in my chest, and I'm not sure if it's at the threat of war or the fact that her using the word love has me grinning like a damn fool.

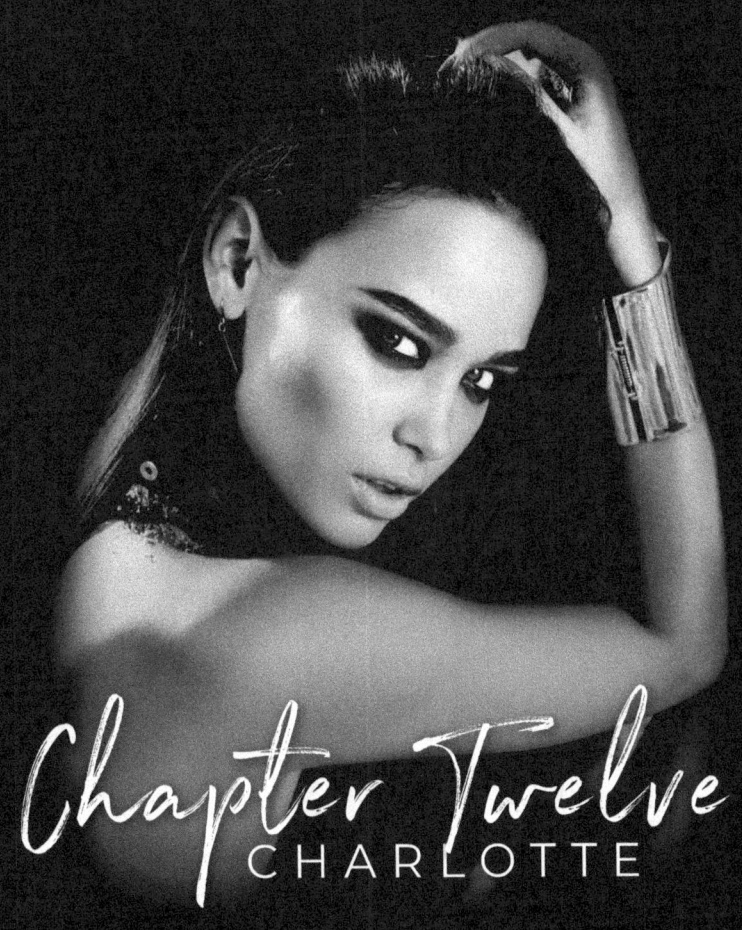

Chapter Twelve

CHARLOTTE

Collapsing onto the bed, I can't help but press my fingers to my lips, my body shuddering as I remember the taste of his mouth. The scent of cloves and cinnamon envelop my senses and like an addict looking for her next hit, I'm dying to taste his lips once more.

My fingers plunge into the wetness of my mouth and I stifle a groan. Imagining it's his tongue swirling with mine, I let my hand wander, reveling in how intense everything feels.

Wet fingers trail down my neck and over the peak of my breast, brushing against an erect nipple and sending a jolt straight to my clit. I find myself biting my lip in an attempt to keep my noise level down, not wanting Aiden to hear how our almost kiss has left me reeling.

Traveling further south, I let myself feel the lace of my panties and how coarse they are against the pads of my soft fingers. Sliding the thin material to the side, I'm immediately met with my wetness, a flush of warmth rushing through me as one digit slowly strokes between the folds.

Gasping as I hit that little bundle of nerves, my thighs clench together, needing more.

The thought of his expansive chest and those impressively strong arms hovering over me as he plunges his cock deep inside me has me shaking. That very image compelling me to follow through with my fingers as I plunge in and out of my pussy, adding friction to my clit with the base of my palm.

My free hand flies up to my mouth, biting down and groaning as my vision blurs and a kaleidoscope of colors flash before me. A strangled moan escapes me and I can't find two fucks to give as I come down from the highest of highs.

All from my hand and an image of the man of my dreams.

Far too soon, the darkness of guilt washes over me. *What have I done?!* I've just fantasized about someone who's been inside my own sister!

Disgust at myself has me rolling over, burying my face in a pillow. What kind of sick and twisted person lusts after their sister's ex?

Soft rapping at the door has me bolting out of the bed and stumbling onto the floor, the loud thump impossible to deny.

"Char—" Aiden's eyes go wide as he sees me on the floor. Following his gaze, I see what he sees—an exposed breast, and a dress hiked up past my panty line where my lace thong is askew. He looks away, giving me a moment to compose myself, but the bulge in his pants is hard to miss. "I'm sorry. I heard the thump and got worried."

My face burns as I right myself, fumbling to stand. "Um, right. Well, I was just... uh..." Blowing out a breath, I give it up. There's no doubt in my mind he knows what I was up to. "Did you need me?"

He chokes on his own saliva before finally returning his gaze to me. *Right, I probably could've worded that better.*

"I was coming to let you know that the boys will be arriving with Sylvie shortly. I've ordered from Renzetti's tonight so we can all eat together without having to bother with cooking." His brow arches, a playful smile replacing the nervous smirk. "Do you know how to cook, Charlotte?"

My jaw drops and eyes narrow, "Of course I know how to cook!" *If boiling pasta counts as cooking, then yes. I can cook. But he doesn't need to know that right now.* Lord knows I don't need any more humiliation after what he just witnessed.

I may be in a safe house, but the last thing I want is for him to see me as some helpless damsel.

"Daddddyyyyyyy!!!!" Two blond little boys come barreling into the room and practically slam into the wall of man standing before me.

"Oof! You got me!" Aiden acts as if the twins have the power to bring him down, and in a way, I suppose they do. Nothing but adoration floods his eyes as he looks down at his children. "Boys,

89

I want you to meet a very dear friend of mine. Charlotte, this is Matt and this is Max."

Both sets of eyes swing to me, and just like that, I'm their sole focus. Their little eyes going wide before beginning their assault.

"Wow, you sure are pretty."

"Are you staying here too?"

"Do you work with our daddy?"

"Are you Bella's friend?"

"How old are you?"

"Boys, boys. Enough. There will be time to catch up. But for now, how about we let Sylvie get you settled into your room?" Turning toward the door, I see a silver-haired lady smiling and giving me a knowing look.

The look on her face tells me she sees right through me, and I quickly glance down, making sure I haven't accidentally left myself disheveled. *Nope. All good.* Breathing a sigh of relief, I shift where I stand, uncomfortable with the idea of having to endure any more embarrassment for today.

"Does that mean we get to share a room?!" Matt shrieks in excitement as Max jumps up and down.

I can't help but grin at their enthusiasm, it undoubtedly rubbing off on me as I stare into their joyful faces.

"Yes. You get to share a room, it's the first one on the right when you reach the top of the stairs. Sylvie, do you mind taking them? Titus already brought some of their things over."

"Of course, sir. You need not ask." The matronly woman grabs either boys' hand and directs them out of the room. "Come on, gremlins, we have some unpacking to do."

"Ahhhhh, do we have to?" Both little heads fall as they drag their feet out the door, and I chuckle.

"What's so funny?" Aiden's face is stone-cold serious, and I have to wonder if he's joking.

"Oh, just that they have a billionaire father yet they're still expected to unpack their own things. I like it. I like it *a lot*."

"Do you, now?" He stalks toward me, like a hunter hunting its prey. Slowly but deliberately, his steps bring him to me—my dark knight. "I can make you unpack your things too, if you'd like."

I gasp as his lips brush the shell of my ear, "Funny. I didn't bring anything."

His hands slide around my waist, squeezing me against him.

"But I did, *principessa*." His nose trails down my neck, inhaling deeply and letting out a groan. "There's a bag with a few of your things on the chair behind me. I'll always take care of you, little one."

The back of my knees hit the edge of the bed, and it's just now that I've realized he's been slowly walking me backward. Lowering me on the bed, my thoughts immediately shift to the boys

"The door. It isn't locked," I pant, my breathing ragged.

"Everyone's upstairs and they know to knock. So *can I?*" His right hand trails the curves of my collarbone as the other cradles me possessively.

I shake my head, trying to clear it from this fog it's in. "Can you what?"

"Take care of you, *principessa?*" His amber eyes seer into my soul, seeing right through any pretense I may have been holding on to.

Slowly, I nod, giving myself to him.

"I need to hear your words, baby. I'm not going to do something you don't want." His gaze begins to harden, and it takes every ounce of restraint not to jump all over him.

I *do not* want him breaking free of this bubble we're in. The world might be crumbling around us and this might be ten shades of fucked up, but there's no doubt that I want him with every fiber of my being.

My hand reaches up, scraping the stubble across his jaw and he visibly shudders. "I want this, Aiden. I want you. I've always wanted you."

Sucking in a sharp breath, he begins to trail both hands down my chest, over my stomach and onto my thighs, ending his journey down my body at my knees. With one swift movement, he's got me spread open before him and the look in his eyes could only be described as hunger.

Biting my lip, I moan in frustration. If he doesn't do something fast, I'm bound to erupt from his stare alone.

I need friction, I need touch, I need—"Aaahhh."

His finger runs up my seam and I almost come undone right then and there.

Decades I've dreamed of this man. Always forbidden, always just a dream. But now, here he is in front of me and he's touching me with such reverence in his eyes, I'm about to burst, overwhelmed with emotion.

"You like that, princess?" His lips curl into a smug smile.

He knows what he's doing to me, and he's enjoying every second of it.

Rolling my eyes, I go to swat his hand away but his reflexes are too fast. He captures my wrist, bringing it to his mouth and nipping at the flesh, sending a bolt of heat flashing right through me.

He lowers himself to my core, inhaling what he does to me, "God, Charlotte. You're so damn beautiful."

Before I can respond, he's moved the lace to the side, gently sucking on my nub and sending my head falling backward onto the bed. My hands grab at the comforter, trying to grab hold of anything solid.

The room is spinning, my world is tilting, and everything I ever thought was real has shifted. This man's mouth is magic. Nothing short of fucking magic.

Just as I start to adjust to the sensation of his lips on me, Aiden takes two fingers and thrusts them into me, giving me the fullness my body was craving. His fingers and mouth are relentless, giving me pleasure I never thought possible.

My body begins to vibrate as a coil of overwhelming sensation begins to spread from my core down to my toes and I know I'm close.

One last suck and nip at my clit and I'm falling down the dark hole of bliss, never wanting to leave.

Lying here on this bed, I know I've never been happier, and I want to revel in this moment forever.

A soft kiss to my mound has me opening my eyes—*I hadn't even realized they were closed*—and what I see has my insides crumbling.

Aiden's face is back to its cold and indifferent state. What happened? Oh my god, does he regret this? Does he hate himself for being with me? I fidget with my dress trying to lower it, heat rising to my cheeks and it's not from the mind-blowing orgasm I just experience.

"Why don't you get yourself ready for dinner. Your clothes and a few personal items are by the door. Let me know if you need anything else and I'll have one of the men run out and get it." His hands trail the outside of my thighs, and though his touch is gentle and sweet, his face is still cold and hard.

I need to know what happened, and I've never been one to leave well enough alone. "Aiden, did I do something wrong?"

"No, princess. You're nothing but perfect. It was me who stepped out of line." He gets up, running a hand through his ebony hair. "I saw you on the floor, caught in the middle of an intimate moment, and something came over me. I needed to take care of you, make you feel something other than the shit you've been feeling."

He looks away, and I don't know if the look in his eyes is rage at what's happened to me or what he's allowed himself to do.

"Aid—"

"No, Charlotte. What that man did to you is unforgivable. What *I* did to you just now is also unforgivable."

"Stop. Do not compare your actions to those of Preston's. What you did was give me pleasure. What he has done is bring me nothing but pain."

"But it's not my place to do that, and you know it." He strides to the door, opening it wide before looking back. "Please be ready in twenty minutes. The boys have a strict bedtime schedule and I'd like to adhere to it."

And just like that, our moment is broken.

Over a decade of pining after a man, and for what? To ruin it all for just one quick frolic in bed?

Fuck that. I want more. I need more, and I'll do whatever it takes to get it.

Chapter Thirteen
AIDEN

Storming into the kitchen, I see Titus peer up from his phone. "Don't give me that look."

"Who knew that when I offered to bring the twins and Sylvie, I'd get dinner *and* a show." He sucks in his lips, fighting the smile that's visible despite his efforts.

I shoot him a glare that would make a lesser man cower. Apparently, Titus has a death wish.

"Oh, come on. You can't blame me for poking some fun. I called it from day one. The way you looked at her, like she hung the moon... it was only a matter of time before you two were playing hide the salami."

"Shut your mouth before I make you. She's a married woman and we are doing no such thing." I bury my face into the takeout bags that arrived while I was *busy* with Charlotte.

"Oh, so those groans I heard were a figment of my imagination. Good to know I call out *your* name while imagining a good ol romp in the sheets."

I toss a breadstick at Titus' head, but of course he catches it. Bastard's reflexes are almost as good as mine. *Almost.*

"Food fight!" My two little terrors run into the kitchen and dive into the bags of food.

"No food fight tonight, boys." I muss their hair before grabbing the bags and bringing them to the table. "Come sit. I ordered your favorites."

"Yes! Did you get the tiramisu?" Max licks his lips in anticipation. That boy definitely got my sweet tooth.

"You know it, little man." I pull the boxes containing their spaghetti and meatballs, placing one in front of each of them. "But no dessert before dinner, so eat up."

Amidst the grumbling, I hear a gasp. Looking up, I see a very flushed Charlotte, her gaze falling on Titus.

"Hello Titus. I didn't know you were here. Is everything okay?" She's flustered, and it's so damn adorable.

"Yes, I've been here a while." He smirks and I kick him under the table. "Oof. Damn Aiden, you wearing those steel tipped boots again?"

At his words, Charlotte's face visibly pales and she stumbles forward.

Bolting out of my chair, I'm at her side in two seconds flat. "Are you okay? You should probably sit and eat something. It's been an intense twenty-four hours."

"She can sit next to us!" Matt belts out, scooching his brother over to make room for Charlotte. I guess all Moretti men have a soft spot for this brunette beauty.

"What, am I chopped liver now?" Nanny Silvie walks into the kitchen, teasing the boys like she always does.

"We still love you, Miss Sylvie. But Miss Charlotte is special."

Bless our nanny, she doesn't take offense at my boy's words, she simply smiles and pats him on the head. "I suppose she is, isn't she?" As if under attack, she throws me a knowing smirk and I can't help but feel that the universe is conspiring to dissolve what little willpower I have left.

I already feel like a piece of shit for doing what I did with Charlotte, but seeing her on the floor like that—something in me just snapped.

In that moment, I wanted to be her sole source of pleasure. That's right. I was jealous of her own damn hand. That's a new low for me.

Never have I desired a woman so much that I was jealous of her own appendages.

"It smells so good in here. Can I help with anything?" Charlotte takes a seat between both boys. Smart woman. The way those two are looking at her, I wouldn't put it past them to fight over who she sat next to.

"It's Renzetti's dear. The best Italian food in the whole of DFW." Sylvie serves Charlotte a helping of the lasagna, some salad and of course the bread—which happens to be my favorite.

Renzetti's is owned by the infamous Renzetti *Famiglia* based out of New York. They are the real deal, and their food is no different.

"Well, it smells absolutely divine." She takes the bread stick and puts it in her mouth, and I can't help it, my fucking cock twitches.

"Stare any harder and I might accuse you of having a food fetish." Titus whispers behind his drink.

I give him a glance and he makes a motion with his hand as if he were zipping his mouth. *Good.* I don't need to worry about his childish jokes upsetting Charlotte. She doesn't need anymore distress in her life and knowing the type of humor Titus enjoys, there's no doubt it would somehow offend her.

"So dear, tell me about yourself?" Sylvie looks at Charlotte, curiosity peppering her normally placid expression.

"Nothing much to say, really. I'm just your typical southern belle. Born and raised in Dallas, attended college here, and—" She stabs at her salad, whatever else she was going to say dies on her lips. "Anyway, my family lives here so I guess it's a good thing I do too."

"Oh, that's wonderful. It must be nice to be so close to your family. My daughter lives in the UK. I try to visit when I can, but being so far away is hard on us both. Especially now that she's expecting."

My heart clenches, and I know it's only a matter of time before Nanny Sylvie leaves us to care for her own daughter. I know we'll all miss her.

"Congratulations on the new grandbaby! That is so exciting, to have little ones in the family."

Sylvie glances my way before asking Charlotte her next question, "What about you, dear? Would you like to have a family of your own?"

Charlotte's cheeks flush, but she answers as if unfazed, "Yes. I'd love a family of my own. Unfortunately, I'm not currently at a place in my life where that will be happening anytime soon." She lets out a scoff. "No, my sister is much closer to that milestone in her life. Speaking of which, I don't have a phone with me. Is it possible to borrow your phone, Aiden? I'd like to let her know I'm no longer living in Highland Park."

I clear my throat before answering, knowing I'll probably be met with some resistance. "About that, I don't think it's in your best interest to talk to anyone outside of our team right now. At least until you've talked to your lawyer."

As the realization of my words hits her, she lets her fork fall to the table, its metal grip clanking on the plate. "I'm sorry, but that sounds an awful lot like control to me and I didn't just escape the grasp of one man's hold to fall into that of another's." Looking around the table, she realizes she's had an emotional outburst in front of other people, and knowing my *principessa perfetta*, that's not something she allows herself to do. *Ever.* She pushes away from the table, the legs of the chair scraping against the hardwood floor. "If you'll excuse me, I'm not feeling very hungry. Boys, I promise we'll spend more time together tomorrow morning."

Oh no, she doesn't. If she thinks she can make a statement like that and then simply walk away, she has another thing coming. Getting up from my chair I tell Sylvie I'll be right back. With a smile and a wink, she nods in agreement.

It's time to bring my principessa down from that mountain of fury she's on.

Charlotte

The audacity of that man! As if he hasn't been privy to all of the torture I've endured with Preston. Where does he get off thinking that he can order me around and take my phone privileges away like I'm some teenager?

I go to slam the door, but thick fingers gripping the edge of the door stop me.

"Not so fast, principessa. Our conversation isn't over."

I lick my lips as the vein in his forearm beckons my eyes. I don't know what it is about him, but even his forearms are sexy to me. All that power... *focus, Charlotte, you're supposed to be mad at him.*

"Like what you see, mia principessa piccolina?" His brow lifts and his lips curl upward into a sly smile.

"No. I was just looking at your damn hand, trying to control me yet again. Don't think that with your sexy smirk you can make me forget what you've done."

"So you think my smirk is sexy?" I let out a breath of frustration as he slowly backs me into the room, closing the door behind him. "Okay, okay. Let's talk about it. What exactly upset you? I hope you know that everything I'm doing is to keep you safe."

Sitting on the bed, I give in to my anger, letting him have every single thought raging in my head. "You want to know what's my problem? I'll tell you what's my problem. For as long as I can remember, there's always been someone trying to control everything I do. The clothes I wear, the music I listen to, the books I read, the people I associate with, the schools I've gone to, and *yes,* even the man I married. *No more!* I've had enough! From now on I want to live for me and do only the things I want, be with whoever I want, and most certainly talk to whoever I want. So, there. I will not let you control me and if you try to do it, you're just as bad as Preston and I'll have to leave."

Before I know what I'm doing, I'm up walking toward the small bag of clothing Aiden brought me. In my head, I'm getting what little belongings I have and hightailing it out of here. Apparently, Aiden has other plans.

Walking behind me, Aiden slides both of his hands down either side of my waist and gently brings my back to his chest. "Shhh, *piccolina.* There's no need to get all flustered. Like I was saying, I'm just trying to keep you safe, not control you. There's a difference. How about I tell you why I think it can impair your safety and you can tell me if you still think I'm acting against your best interest, hm?"

Damn him and his being reasonable. Melting into his back, I slowly nod. He turns us so he's sitting on the chair and lowers me onto his lap.

"Let's look at the facts. There's no disputing that Preston is a very powerful man. He has influence over many, and we don't know how far that reach extends. One innocent call to your sister where you inadvertently release a bit of information that can clue him in as to where you are and it can bring him to our very doorstep." I go to speak, but he gently puts his thumb on my mouth, softly stroking the sensitive skin back and forth. "Hold on, I know what you're probably going to say. 'But my sister won't tell anyone anything about our conversation.' That may be true, but like I said before, Preston has influence. Who's to say that he hasn't tapped your sister's phone? For all we know, he'd be listening in and something so innocent can quickly spiral into something dark and dangerous."

My body shivers in his arms, and he notices, bringing me closer to his chest. "Okay, that makes sense. But I can't hold off on talking to my own sister forever. She'll likely start to worry. I know our relationship doesn't seem like it's all that great, but I know she loves me. In her own way, at least."

"I'm not asking that you cut off communication indefinitely—just until we talk to your lawyer. He will likely put things in place so we'd at least have legal recourse if Preston tried anything."

"Okay." I nibble on my lower lip, knowing I need to apologize but not wanting to. Let's just say it's not where my strength lies. "I'm sorry I compared you to Preston. You two are *very* different men and comparing you to each other is like comparing apples to oranges."

"There's no need to apologize. You've just escaped from a very traumatizing situation. It's no wonder that my actions made you react the way you did. It was my fault, I should have approached the subject with a little more tact."

I don't think he was tactless at all, but the fact that he's willing to bear the burden for some of the blame speaks volumes.

No, this man is very different. Very different, indeed.

Chapter Fourteen
AIDEN

The smell of something burning has me running into the kitchen where I find a flustered Charlotte and two grinning boys to either side of her.

Taking in the scene, my heart stutters. Despite the chaos of flour everywhere and dirty dishes piled on the counter, the boys look so content and I could see this becoming commonplace... well, minus the plumes of smoke coming from the waffle maker.

"I thought you said you could cook," I tease Charlotte, knowing it will make her blush that beautiful shade of pink.

"I miiiiight have stretched the truth a little." She shrugs her shoulders as she wipes the back of her hand across her forehead, leaving a trace of batter behind.

Unable to help myself, I walk over and remove it with my thumb, making sure to suck it off for the benefit of her hungry eyes. The way they linger on my mouth lets me know she's dying for a repeat of last night. And to be honest, so am I.

But we can't. I need to double down on what strength I possess to keep myself from touching her.

"Miss Charlotte is helping us make waffles, dad." Max smiles so wide I can practically count all of his teeth.

"Is that so? And who's idea was this?"

"Mine." Charlotte wrings the napkin in front of her, averting my gaze. "I told Sylvie she could take the morning off and that I'd handle breakfast. It was a little ambitious of me, but I wanted to help with something. I can't just sit here all day and not contribute in any way."

"Oh, I can find a couple of things for you to do." My voice lowers as a finger trails down her back, and I immediately reprimand myself for playing this way. It definitely won't lead to anything good, and all it's doing is leading poor Charlotte on. "I'm sorry about that. It was out of line. What I meant to say was that there is plenty for you to do here if you'd like to help. But how about we leave the cooking to the experts?" I grab her hand and walk her to the other side of the counter, plopping her down on one of the barstools before taking my place between the twins. "What do you say, boys? Want to help me make Miss Charlotte some French toast and bacon?"

"I get to crack the eggs!" Matt beelines it to the fridge pulling out the carton as we all chuckle, the merriment of the room making me see this is something worth fighting for—lazy mornings with these three is definitely something I could get used to.

Charlotte

The lawyer Aiden hired was able to make a house call, something I'm extremely grateful for. Despite my willingness to leave the house yesterday, I'm not quite ready to face the outside world just yet.

"Mrs. Ruther—"

"Please, call me Charlotte." I cringe hearing my married name. I don't want to be associated with that asshole one second longer than necessary, and that definitely means dropping his last name like a rotten hot potato.

Mr. Thompson smiles knowingly as he sits back in the wingback chair across from mine.

"Charlotte then. It's not my customary practice to make house calls, but I understand we have a bit of a special situation here." He looks over at Aiden who's made sure to join us for this meeting per my request. He has a shrewd mind, and I'd like him in on what we discuss. Besides, he already knows most of the facts.

"We appreciate you coming in to speak with Charlotte, Jacob." Aiden doesn't smile, ever the stoic presence in the room, but I see the gratitude in his eyes.

"Anything for the men of WRATH. Y'all have been very instrumental in a lot of my cases. The least I could do is come and help a friend in need." Turning back toward me, his expression does a full one-eighty—from joyous to concerned. "Now, to business. It is my understanding the senator has been physical with you on multiple occasions and we actually have evidence of him doing this on video. Normally this type of evidence wouldn't be admissible if the accused hadn't given consent to be recorded in a setting that would have been deemed private. However, because he hired the security firm, it explicitly states in their agreement that surveillance was to be installed throughout the home. This is our loophole around any possible claim that would bar its use in court."

"So, what you're saying is that millions of women across the world can't surreptitiously record evidence of their husbands beating the shit out of them because it's an abuse of their partner's privacy?! That's absolutely insane!" My voice pitches and I have to remind myself that I'm still a lady, despite the shit show I'm currently in.

"In most cases, they can try to admit the evidence, but if the accused has a good lawyer who can dispute the admissibility of the evidence, then no. The jury would not be allowed to see it. It would boil down to the victim's word versus that of the accused."

My blood boils at the injustice of it all, and I make myself a promise to do something to change this. As long as I have breath in me, I will fight for a woman's right to defend themselves against the monsters of this world.

"Char?" Aiden's voice pulls me out of my thoughts. Blinking my eyes, I see that both men are looking at me expectantly.

"I'm sorry. I missed the question, if there was one. What were you saying, Mr. Thompson?"

"It's okay. We can take a break if you need a moment." His sympathetic eyes narrow as his brows scrunch together like two furry caterpillars and it takes everything in me not to giggle.

"No. I'm fine, thank you. Please, let's continue."

"Very well. I was stating that our next move depends on what you'd like the outcome to be. So, what is your dream scenario, Charlotte?"

Taking a deep breath, I close my eyes and speak the words I've felt for so long, "I want to be free."

Aiden reaches over and squeezes my shoulder, the warmth from his grip radiating down my body and making me feel whole.

Opening my eyes, I give him a small reassuring smile before turning back to Mr. Thompson, "What I would like to do is to be free of the senator as quickly as possible."

"I see. Well then, I suggest we move forward with filing for a dissolution of marriage. We will keep it as quiet as possible, but I can't promise anything given the senator's position and the fact that we don't know how he will respond to being served with papers."

A vision of Preston flinging a document at the process server has my stomach roiling. Needing to get the image out of my head, I quickly change the subject.

"I wanted to ask... What is your take on speaking to mutual friends. My sister, specifically." Yes, I understand that referring to my sister as a mutual friend is pretty fucked up. Family should have your back, always, but Clara and I never had that type of relationship.

"I would refrain from talking to anyone until we have a protective order in place. Until then, if you must speak with someone who might be connected to the senator, keep things vague and brief."

Out of my periphery I can see Aiden clenching his jaw, his displeasure evident. *Well, tough shit.* I'm not going to let anyone keep me from what little family I do have.

"Okay, so now that we know what I want, where do we go from here?"

"My office will work on getting the appropriate petition filed as well as securing a protective order and getting the senator served. In the meantime, please be aware of your surroundings and who you talk to." Mr. Thompson turns toward Aiden before continuing. "But I know you are in capable hands with the men of WRATH on the job. You know my daughter still asks about you, right Aiden?"

Aiden's bronzed skin flushes a deeper shade and something in me stirs. *Does he have a history with her?*

"Please send her my regards. I'm glad she's doing well." Aiden's tone is flat, but his skin is still betraying his emotions.

"I will, but you can tell her yourself when you see her at the wedding." Mr. Thompson rises from his chair as he turns his attention back to me. "Charlotte, we'll be sending over a copy of our agreement and be in touch with any updates. If you have any questions in the meantime, please don't hesitate on reaching out to me or my staff. We are at your service."

"Thank you again for your help. I look forward to putting all of this behind me." Squeezing this man's hand, I see the recognition in his eyes. *He understands.* One broken soul acknowledging another.

The weight of his stare almost makes me forget about his daughter. *Almost.*

Chapter Fifteen
AIDEN

"**D**on't you think you're being a little extreme, Aiden?" Titus, the assholiest of ass holes among our group is giving me grief over insensitivity.

"I don't think it's extreme when it comes to her safety. I'll do whatever it takes to keep her safe, even if it means saving her from herself. If I were in Preston's shoes, at risk of losing her, it wouldn't be outside my realm of morals to tap her sister's phone."

"Brother, listen to what you're saying. You are *not* her husband, and she is not yours to protect in that way. Sure, we were hired to keep her safe, but your duties have to stop somewhere. I seems to me you're crossing some lines right here." He taps his hand over his heart and I have to laugh out loud.

"You are insane if you think I have any ulterior motives on keeping her from calling her sister." My hand clenches and Titus doesn't miss it.

Lifting both of his hands in a placating gesture, he tries to reword his previous statement. "All I'm saying is that you seem to care for this broad, and that's not like you. A job is just a job. You never get pulled in and think with your heart. But with this girl, it's like she has a hold on you."

I shake my head, unwilling to even entertain what he's suggesting. She's Clara's little sister. I never slept with her, but I sure as hell did plenty. The fact that I forgot about all that, and dove face-first into Charlotte's delicious folds should give me pause.

It should. But it doesn't.

"Shake your head all you want but the facts speak for themselves." It's his turn to shake his head as he mumbles under his breath. "Another one bites the dust."

"Who bit the dust?" Charlotte walks into the kitchen, glancing at the table where Titus and I are sitting.

"Nobody. Titus is making up stories in his head." Rubbing my hand over my face, I attempt to change the uncomfortable mood in the air. "Have you checked your email? Thompson sent over the agreement as well as a copy of the protective order."

"Oh!" Charlotte puts down the glass of water she'd just filled. "That means I can call my sister, right?"

Titus has the balls to chuckle. Shooting him a death stare, I answer. "I'd really rather you not, but if you feel it's necessary then I'd like to listen in to make sure nothing gives away our location."

Charlotte's entire demeanor changes. From warm and cheerful to cold and closed off. "I'm a grown woman who knows how to conduct herself discreetly. I don't think I need a chaperone to talk to my sister."

"Last time I checked, I was the security expert here." I stare right into her mocha eyes, daring her to fight me, but Titus breaks our contact.

"Okaaaay, I'll leave you two love birds to it. If you need me, I'll be a phone call away." With a salute, Titus makes his exit.

Coming at me, Charlotte's full five-foot-three looms over my chair, pointing her index finger into my chest. "If you think you can control who I talk to, you are dead wrong. I'm done with people telling me who I can and can't talk to. If you have a problem with that then maybe I need to hire someone else for the job."

My nostrils flare and my breathing speeds up. "Listen here, Charlotte. You can throw your little tantrum, but if I tell you I'm going to do something, then damn it, I'm going to do it. I'm one of the best in my field, and I'll do everything in my power to keep you safe. That includes putting up with your tantrums and bullheaded ass."

Her mouth slacks open and my dick can't help but twitch, thinking of all the naughty things that little mouth of hers can do. As if my hand has a mind of its own, my thumb traces the contours of her lips before plunging into her wet mouth.

Charlotte closes her lips around me, sucking with nothing but sheer hunger in her eyes, her tongue swirling around my digit before withdrawing it and biting the tip.

Growling, I place my hands on her hips, bringing her down onto my lap with either leg straddling me. As soon as her apex hits the bulge in my pants, Charlotte lets out a whimper.

Knowing what she needs, I begin to rock her into my length, giving her that sweet friction she's after.

"Aiden..."

My name on her lips sends a current of warmth rushing through me, making my chest expand and melting my icy heart. "Yes, princess?"

"You feel so *fucking* good." A mewl at the end of her claim has me attacking her mouth with uncharted desperation. I need to taste her like I need air. Our lips and teeth clash, needing to consume every bit of passion between us, chasing that fleeting moment of rightness before the darkness of our reality destroys our bliss.

"Mmm, baby." Dragging my lips from her mouth, I nip at her jaw before continuing my path down her neck and biting.

"Ahh. More." Her words come out in a hushed pant as she grinds herself on me, stopping and rocking forward when her center meets my tip—the pressure of which sends me spiraling into a needy pile of man, feral and hungry and not giving a damn about our situation or our surroundings.

Grabbing her by the ass, I lift her and carry her to the counter, making her sun dress ride up past her thighs and exposing the drenched lace that lies underneath. *Fuck. I'm a goner.*

The evidence of her desire lies before me, and if I had any shred of reservations, this shuts it down.

Charlotte locks eyes with me, her small hand stroking me over my pants. Once. Twice. And then a third before sliding inside my slacks, her soft skin caressing my hard length and causing a bead of precum to escape.

Licking her lips, Charlotte bends forward giving me a delicious view of her gorgeous tits. *Full and round, perfect for sucking.*

Pulling me further into this hurricane of lust and emotion, Charlotte's lips reach the exposed tip of my cock, her pink tongue peeking out and licking the wetness from my slit.

Like a beast that's lost all control, I growl, grabbing her by the shoulders and lowering her back down on the granite. Charlotte props herself up on her forearms as her eyes follow my hands, tracing down her torso past her thighs and down to her knees where I spread her open wide.

Taking my hand, I set myself free, giving myself two hard and hungry pumps before bringing my throbbing cock to her lace.

I stroke her over the fabric, the sensation and friction causing her to arch her back and moan.

"Daaaaddddyy!!!!" A tiny voice breaks into our bubble of lust.

"Shit." I mumble as I tuck myself back in and Charlotte lowers her dress just in time.

"Max won't share his tablet!" Matt runs into the kitchen, his face red from having been running. No doubt chasing his brother in an attempt to retrieve the damn tablet.

Letting out a breath of frustration, I keep my body facing the counter. The last thing I need is to traumatize anyone with a view of my aching erection.

Charlotte catches on, hops off the counter and faces my boy. "How about I help you go look for yours? That way you won't have to use your brothers. Hmm?"

Matt beams up at Charlotte as if she were a superhero. "Sounds like a plan."

I chuckle. He can sound like such a grownup sometimes that it makes me miss the days when he was so little he fit right in my arm, like a little baby football.

Babies. What the fuck was I thinking!? Not only was I just about to fuck Clara's little sister in the kitchen where anyone could have walked in on us, but I was about to go in bareback.

My father would be rolling over in his grave. If he taught us anything, it was to always wrap it up. Moretti men have been hunted by hungry women, trying to get their claws into our family fortune. A baby wouldn't be beneath many of them.

Shaking my head, I give myself a mental slap. I know Charlotte isn't like that, but still. She's a married woman for fuck's sake. The last thing she needs is to get pregnant by another man while undergoing her divorce. What a fucking field day that would be. I can see the headlines now...

Senator's Wife Cheats on Husband and Gets Pregnant with Lover's Baby.

No. I could never do that to her. Nor would I want to give Preston an out like that. The bastard deserves to pay for his actions. *I'll make sure of it.*

ACTS OF REDEMPTION

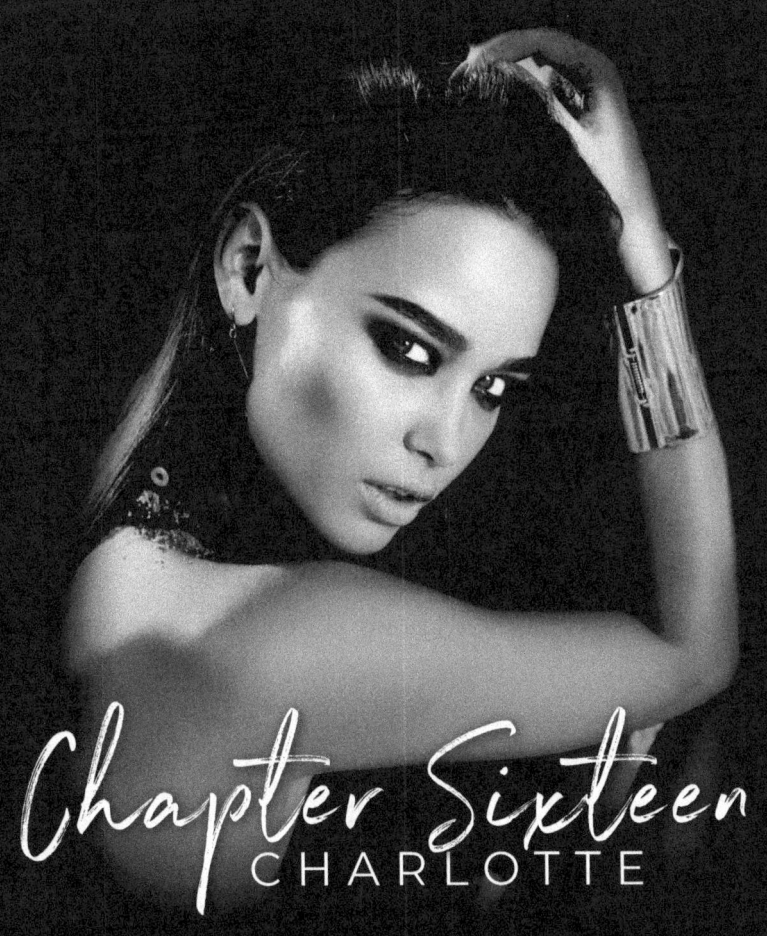

Chapter Sixteen
CHARLOTTE

Those boys have my heart. Even though they are twins, their little personalities couldn't be more different. Matt is studious and loves to spend his time reading on his tablet, while Max is much more of an extrovert, needing to spend his time being the life of the party—even if it's just the five of us in the home.

The five of us. Sylvie, the twins, Aiden, and me. In such a short time, we've sort of developed our own routine—like a real little family. My heart squeezes at the memory of my own family. Never in my life had I felt the warmth and love I do with this new little makeshift family of ours.

My face flushes and I realize that these thoughts are dangerous. This *isn't* my family, and Aiden and I are most certainly *not* together.

Needing to reign in my emotions, I decide to call my real family. Starting with my sister.

The home doesn't have any landline phones, but I know for a fact that Aiden keeps a stash of burner phones in case of emergencies somewhere in the office.

I tiptoe down the hall, leaving the boys in their room. They're too consumed with their games to pay me any mind, and thankfully they don't ask me where I'm going.

The floorboards creak and I groan. Aiden's skills are no exaggeration. He's a SEAL after all, and there's no doubt that if I don't play this right, he'll figure out what I'm up to.

I hear him talking downstairs to Sylvie, something about dinner plans. Good, this is my chance. I tiptoe down the stairs, making sure to stay against the wall so he doesn't see me out of the opening in the kitchen.

Just a few more steps and I'm in the office.

Success!

I close the door behind me as quietly as possible, something that's a major feat in this creaky older home.

The desk is my first guess, but after a thorough search I find nothing. Behind the desk is an antique wooden chest. Opening it slowly, my breath hitches. *Bingo.*

There are passports, cash, and several burner phones.

Picking one up, I try to remember Clara's phone number. Entering the numbers, my heart begins to beat so loudly I feel it throbbing in my ears.

"He—Hello?" Clara's voice comes through the line sounding hesitant.

"Clara? It's Charlotte." My voice is low so as to not call attention. Aiden's hearing is insanely sharp, and I can't have him barging in, cutting me off from my family.

"Char! Oh my god! Where have you been? We are so worried about you!" The *'we'* in her statement have my hackles rising. "Mom asked me to call you about our family gala and when I couldn't get a hold of you, I went to your home only to have Preston's assistant tell me you no longer lived there. I was sure she had to be pulling my leg, but when I couldn't get a hold of Preston either, I started to really worry. Are you okay? Why are you whispering?"

The concern in her voice warms my heart. I knew she cared, even if it was in her own messed up and twisted way.

"Yes, I'm fine. I'm not supposed to talk to anyone right now until things are settled, but I just wanted to tell you that I'm okay."

The door creaks open and I immediately drop the phone to my lap.

"I called Tyler's and placed the same order as al—" Aiden turns his head and finally looks into the room, his words hanging mid sentence as he sees me behind his desk. "Char? What are you doing in here?"

Not wanting Clara to hear our conversation, I quickly end the call without looking up. Aiden's eyes narrow as he rounds the corner of the desk, his eyes falling to my lap and the phone I have clutched in my hand.

Closing his eyes, he lets out a deep breath before opening them once more. "Who did you call, Char?"

Not wanting to back down on what I know is my right, I answer, full bravado in effect. "I told you, I was going to call Clara and I wouldn't let anyone tell me otherwise. I'm done with letting people control me."

Aiden closes his eyes slowly, rubbing his hand over his face. Extending his hand out, he asks for the phone still white-knuckled by my hand. "Please, Char. I want to see the damage we potentially need to recover from."

I hand it over to him, not seeing what the big deal is. It's just Clara.

Aiden looks through the phone and sighs. "A lot could have been said in this time frame and since I don't know exactly what was said then we'll need to take precautions as if you've compromised our location. Yes, Preston knows of the divorce filing, but we still don't know how he will be responding to this new development."

Bolting up from my chair, I get right up in his face. "I was extremely careful and I'll tell you exactly what I said if it will get you to stop acting like an overprotective Neanderthal. I get that we don't want Preston knowing where I am, but this is just too extreme. You're taking me out of one jail and putting me in another, and I just can't take it." My eyes well up with unshed tears, my chest vibrating with rage and hurt all mixed together, slowly bubbling up my throat and ending in a choked sob.

Aiden takes me into his arms, his lips falling to the top of my head. "I'm sorry you're having to go through this, *principessa*. I promise it won't always be like this. If I'm an overprotective Neanderthal, it's because I couldn't stand to see you hurt again. Everything I'm doing it's to keep you safe."

I press my face against his hard chest, the proximity to his body sending a shiver running through me. "Please, Aiden. No running. I swear I said nothing that would give our location away. I've grown fond of our routine here. It brings me peace, something I haven't had in a very long time."

Looking up into his cashmere eyes, I see his warring thoughts. Finally letting out a sigh, he brings his lips to my forehead. "If this home brings you peace, then I won't deny you, little one."

"Thank you." I whisper into his shirt before pressing a kiss over his heart.

Aiden

I know staying here is going against my better judgment, but when she looks up at me with those big brown eyes, there's no denying her.

God, if we ever have a little girl I'll be in big trouble.

A pang of guilt hits me, thinking of Bella and how I never gave her the attention she needed growing up. I was on one tour after another, and whatever little time I would be home, I'd be mentally recovering from whatever mission we'd just completed.

Suddenly the realization of what started me on this rabbit hole of guilt hits.

What the fuck am I thinking?

Charlotte and I will not be having babies because there is absolutely no scenario in which we are together. She's Clara's little sister, for goodness' sake. And as if a high-profile divorce won't bring her enough attention already, her being with her sister's ex-boyfriend will only bring her more gossip and shame.

Quickly dislodging her from my embrace, I take two rapid steps back—the change in my demeanor not going unnoticed.

Charlotte's brows come together, her eyes narrowing in confusion. Before she can say anything, I change the subject altogether.

"You said you wanted to help more around the house, right? How about you go help Sylvie set the table for dinner while I finish up some work here."

Charlotte's brows go from furrowed to reaching her hairline in just a few seconds before she schools her features, and now the coldness of my face is reflected back at me. *Good.* She needs to toughen up a bit more. I don't know what conclusions she's come to in her head about us, but I can't have her thinking there's any future there.

There isn't. The sooner she comes to grips with it, the better for the both of us.

My phone vibrates in my pocket just as I'm sitting down behind the desk. Pulling it out, I see William's number flashing across the screen.

"Is Bella okay?" He never calls me on this line, and my mind immediately goes to my pregnant daughter.

"Well, hello to you too, *Dad*." The bastard drags out that last word, knowing it irritates the shit out of me. "Call me that one more time and we'll see just how I welcome you into the family fold." I grit out between clenched teeth while this guy has the audacity to chuckle.

We might all be friends, but if I'm being honest, I'm still not fully over the fact that my thirty-three-year-old friend is marrying my daughter.

"Relax, old man. I'm just teasing. And yes, Bella is okay. I was actually calling to see why you aren't making it to our weekly dinner. I know you're taking a special interest in your current case, but Titus said he'd gladly sub in while you came to spend some family time with us. Bella misses the boys, and you too, I suppose." More chuckling on his part. He thinks he's a damn comedian.

"I can send the boys over with Nanny Sylvie if they want, but I'm not leaving Char."

There's a sharp intake of breath, and I know I've fucked up. No doubt he caught on to my casual mention of her name.

"So it is true. You are attached to this one. Want to talk about it?"

"I'm not attached. I dated her sister when I was younger, and if you must know, yes, I care. But only because I've known her on a personal level."

"Look, your love life is *your* love life. But if emotions begin to compromise your ability to work the case, then I suggest you pull out." He laughs before continuing. "In more ways than one... get it! Oh, I'm good."

"No, you're not. And I already told you, it's not like that with Charlotte. I do care for her, but like a little sister." The words taste like chalk in my mouth as I speak them. Running a hand through my hair, I groan. I hate lying and that was straight up a lie. There's no way I'd tongue down a little sister.

"Mhm, so that's why Titus says you eye fuck her every chance you get. Look man, like I said, whatever you do as far as your love life is your business. We're just worried about how it will affect your judgment."

Immediately, my thoughts go back to whether or not we should remain in this home after Charlotte's phone slipup. Maybe there is some truth to what William is saying.

"I get it, brother, and I appreciate your concern, but I got this under control. This will all be over soon. Charlotte will be back to her normal life, *sans* the prick Preston, and I will be back to my usual grumpy self at your weekly dinners."

"Hopefully this will all be over in time for the wedding. Bella would be devastated if we had to postpone it. You're walking her down the aisle and there's no way we could have the wedding without you."

I press my fingertips to my temple and rub. "I've let that girl down more than I'd care to remember. I won't let her down again. I'll be there, even if it means dragging Charlotte to the wedding."

"Now there's an idea. Why not bring the future Mrs. to the wedding? I'll tell Bella to add the plus-one to the table."

"Not funny, William. If anyone hears you, your words could be misconstrued, making Charlotte look bad."

"Is that what this is about? You don't want her name tarnished? You should know better than anyone that life is short.

There are no guarantees in life and you should grab hold of any opportunity that brings you joy." He sighs into his phone and pauses, continuing after he sees that I'm not chiming in after that bomb of truth he just dropped. "If that's your only worry then that should be something Charlotte decides for herself. Not you. It's her reputation that's on the line and she's a grown-ass woman."

His words of wisdom echo in my mind. If it were only that simple, but it's not. Not only is her reputation at stake, but she's also still married. This is so wrong on so many levels that it wouldn't just be one thing shaming her name, it would be many.

I've messed up a lot in my life, and I sure as hell am not going to let my selfish need for the woman be another one of my mistakes.

Not if I can help it.

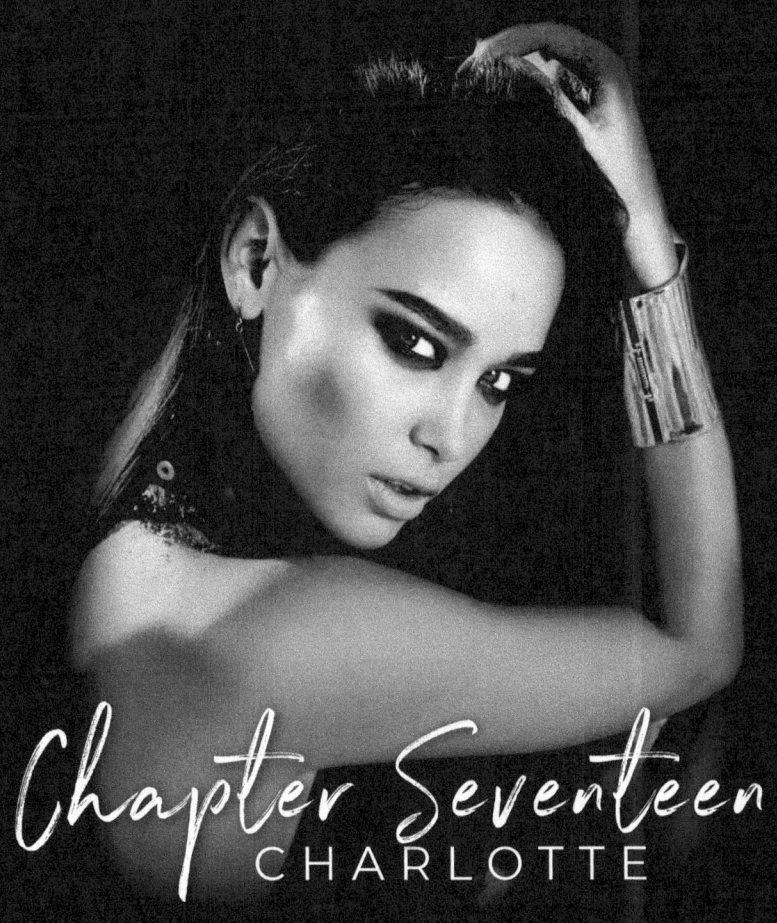

Chapter Seventeen
CHARLOTTE

As I slip the satin and lace nightgown over my head, I smile. Nanny Sylvie gave me a couple of bags containing hand selected items of clothing she thought I'd need and like.

This woman, if I didn't know any better, I'd think she selected these pieces to evoke a reaction out of a particularly grouchy man in this household.

But there's no way. She knows my situation and there's no way Aiden would ever see me in this, right?

Just as I'm about to head to the bed there's a soft knock on the door. Grabbing the matching black satin robe, I loosely wrap it around me before answering it.

My breath halts as I see Aiden standing before me. His gray Henley hugs every muscle as his sweats hang low on his tapered waist, the bulge in his pants making my lady parts clench from the sight alone. He isn't aroused, yet his impressive package of his is enough to create a deliciously large outline of what lies underneath.

Clearing his throat, Aiden chuckles. I squeeze my eyes shut before sighing. I've been caught red-handed ogling my keeper. My cheeks heat and I know I'll have to open my eyes eventually.

"Can I come in for a second?" Aiden's voice cuts through my embarrassment and I finally step aside, refusing to make direct eye contact.

"Of course. What's going on? Has there been word of the senator's wife running away?" I try to make light of the situation, but that isn't really far from the truth.

"No. All's quiet on that front. For now, at least." I see him pacing in front of my bed before he finally lowers himself onto the edge of the mattress, patting the comforter next to him.

Taking a hesitant step toward him, I slowly lower myself to the bed. The sheer proximity of him with both of us dressed in our intimate attire is almost too much for me to bear.

"Okay, so then what?"

Grabbing my hand in his, he squeezes. "I have a favor to ask of you."

His response takes me aback. He's done so much for me, I could never in a million years repay him for what he's given me.

"Of course. I'd do anything to help you, though I'm not sure what I could possibly do for you."

Immediately dirty thoughts race through my mind. Me on my knees before him, taking his length into my mouth, savoring the masculine taste of his... *what is wrong with me?* Here I am, in hiding, and the first thing that comes to mind is giving him a blow job? *Get it together, girl.*

Oblivious to my internal thoughts, Aiden moves on with our conversation. "As you may already know, Bella's wedding is coming up." His face flushes a deep bronzed color, bringing out the gold flecks in his irises. "I haven't always been the best father, that's no secret, and there's just no way I could let her down more than I already have."

"I'm sure you haven't been that bad, Aiden. We always think the worst of ourselves."

He turns his head, hiding his gorgeous eyes from me. Reaching my hand up, I bring his face back to mine. "Hey, don't do that. There's nothing you could say that would change the way I look at you. It might be over a decade since we spent a substantial amount of time together, but I know you." Placing a hand over his heart, I try to channel all of the love I feel. "I know what's in here and it is nothing but solid gold."

Aiden's nostrils flare and his jaw hardens before he takes my hand and brings it to his lips, kissing my palm in one of the most tender shows of affection I've ever received. "How are you so damn perfect, my *piccolina principessa?*"

I shove at him playfully, "How quickly we forget this morning's breakfast blunder."

"Oh no, I haven't forgotten. I just happen to think it adds to your endearment." Grinning like loons, the perfect silence of the moment bursts when Aiden's phone vibrates. Looking down at it, he sighs before shoving it back in his pocket. "That was William, and he wants to know if I have an answer for him, but I can't give it to him until I ask you."

My back straightens and the smile that was plastered all over my face fades. "Okay. What is it?"

"Like I was saying, I haven't been the perfect father to Bella. Her mother died when she was only fifteen, and instead of being there for her, I loaded her up with responsibilities that weren't hers to bear." He rubs the back of his neck, closing his eyes and inhaling deeply. "Any time she would try to bring up anything having to do with emotions, I just shut her out."

Squeezing his hand, I urge him on silently. If he needs to vent, I will be his solace.

"She was caring for the twins as if she were their mom. Instead of doing normal things girls her age did, she was going to soccer and T-ball, carting around two very wild boys. Then, when I got injured, I wasn't able to be there for her for months. Even in the little capacity I had been. William stepped up to the plate and helped her while she helped him with his daughter, Harper. I guess one thing led to another, and they fell in love." His face scrunches on that last bit, cringing at the idea of his friend dating his daughter. "No father wants to hear that their thirty something business partner and friend is sleeping with their eighteen-year-old daughter. Add to that a brain injury where my temper wasn't being regulated properly, and it just spelled disaster."

"It's okay, Aiden. I'm sure she understood." I want to give him comfort, but I don't know what else to do other than place my hands on him, giving him my warmth and letting him know I'm not going anywhere.

"That's not the worst part." He takes a deep breath before looking me dead in the eyes. "I kicked her out of our home. Told her she wasn't a part of my family anymore. And adding insult to injury, I took the boys away from her. Sent them to boarding school while I sorted myself out. Didn't even give her visitor rights." His lips press into a thin line as his eyes begin to shimmer with the promise of tears. "By the time I got my shit together, William had already proposed and months had passed where we hadn't spoken. Yes, I apologized and we've worked on our relationship since then, but I can't afford to lose her again."

"Life is nothing but a collection of moments. Good, bad, beautiful and ugly. It's up to us to cherish those that move us, and release those that no longer serve us." I tighten the grip I have on his forearm before continuing. "You had a severe brain injury. You weren't yourself, and I know without a shadow of a doubt that Bella has moved on from that ordeal. She's your daughter after all, and despite your icy exterior, you are a good human being. Hang on to those good moments and let the rest go. I've seen you with the twins and how you worry about Bella. Trust me, you're also a good father."

The corner of his mouth lifts into an almost smile. *It's something.*

"Thank you for saying that—and I appreciate your words—but I didn't tell you all this to get any sympathy." He gives me a full-on smirk now and I'm graced with his sexy-as-hell dimple.

"Jokes aside, I do want to ask you something and I wanted you to know why this was so important to me first."

"Okay. Spit it out already." Brushing aside a loose strand of hair and tucking it behind my ear, it's my turn to smirk.

"As you already know, Bella and William are getting married. As her father, I'm walking her down the aisle. The thing you haven't been privy to is the date. It's only a couple of weeks away and I have a feeling that the divorce won't be finalized by then, nor will we have the situation between you and Preston secured." His jaw clenches and I know it pains him to say my husband's name.

"So what are you asking?" My brows scrunch together into a unibrow, trying to guess what that could possibly have to do with me.

"I want you to come."

I'm stunned into silence. My face heats up and I know I probably look like a ketchup bottle with how fair my skin is naturally.

"I understand if you don't want—"

I quickly rush to reassure him before he withdraws the invite. "No, no. Of course I want to go. It's just a surprise, that's all. It's such an intimate event. I read in the paper that it's going to be strictly close friends and family."

A small smile touches his lips, the warmth radiating through his whole demeanor. "Yes, and your point is? You fit the category, don't you?" He chuckles and seeing that I'm stunned into silence once more, he takes the reins of our conversation. "Bella has never been one for crowds and after everything that transpired the last year, I don't blame her for wanting to keep it small. So what do you say, are you in?"

"You mean like a date? I would love to be your date, but I don't know if that's the best thing since the divorce won't be final. But if it were after it was final then I would love that. Not that I want your daughter to change her wedding date or something." Sucking in a sharp breath, I roll my lips in and squeeze my eyes shut, trying to stop myself before my treacherous mouth and its verbal diarrhea does what it does best. Shits on something beautiful.

His wide eyes and little smirk tell me he wasn't inviting me as a date, and now I feel like the biggest fool. Thankfully, Aiden steps in before I can say anything else and stick my foot further in my mouth.

"I would love to have you come with me as a date. As you said, though, it's probably not the best timing right now. But we could settle for you coming as a friend, right?"

Dig my hole and bury me now. If it were possible to melt into the ground and have it swallow me whole, I'd gladly take that option. Instead, I give him a curt nod, my lips still rolled in.

"Char, don't be embarrassed. You are such a strong woman, shame doesn't suit you." His strong hand reaches up, the back of his fingers caressing my cheek. "Now, show me that gorgeous smile of yours."

Unable to resist, I give him what he wants. The corners of my lips lift into a timid smile, and my reward is the hunger I see reflected back at me as his gaze devours my mouth. His thumb traces the contours, and it's as if I've forgotten to breathe, anticipating his next move.

Excruciatingly slow, Aiden moves his face closer to mine, his lips hovering over the places his finger just traced—like a supernova reaching the end of its life, an explosion of light is all I see as our lips join into one.

One fluid movement.

One single desire.

One damnable offense.

Chapter Eighteen
AIDEN

T he kiss—this damn kiss—it's enough to have me throwing all sense I once had out the window. Fuck. Out of the damn state of Texas.

Gripping the back of her neck, I deepen the kiss. Needing more of her mouth, more of her breath, more of her petal soft skin. She bites my lip, hard, and I can't help but place both hands on her waist, lifting her up and throwing her toward the center of the bed.

Like a man starving, I set my eyes on the prize, crawling my way up to her. Charlotte's eyes widen and her mouth slightly parts, an audible gasp leaving that perfect mouth of hers.

"Do you want this, principessa?" I want her like a wild animal wants its prey, but there is no way I will take what is not freely given.

A wicked smile spreads across her face before she grabs at my shirt, eagerly lifting it up and over my head.

Chuckling, I stare down at her. "Words, baby. I need your words."

"Yes, I've wanted you for as long as I can remember, Aiden. Now please, don't make me beg."

I arch a brow, "Now there's something I could get behind."

Charlotte tries to scurry backward and out from between my legs, but I'm faster. Dropping my body weight on her, she gasps once more, no doubt feeling my length pressing against her apex.

"Shhhh, baby. I was just joking. As you can see—" I roll my hips into her center, eliciting a groan that has me almost coming in my pants. "I want you, and I have no intention of making you beg."

Charlotte wraps her legs around my waist, writhing underneath me, seeking her own release. Lowering the straps to her lace nightgown, I expose her beautiful breasts. Dusky pink nipples greet my hungry eyes and I can't help but bring my mouth down and take one into my mouth, suckling that tender flesh that tastes like heaven and sin combined.

Lifting her toward me, I remove the black satin and realize she isn't wearing any panties. Instantly, my cock jerks into the mattress, demanding entry. *Soon, boy. Soon.*

"So fucking beautiful." My words are a whisper as I look at her body underneath me. Kissing the space between her breasts, I mumble into her soft skin. "But the most beautiful of all is what lies in here."

Her body shivers beneath my kiss and when my eyes travel back up to hers, I see recognition. Unlike anything I've ever experienced, her soul sees mine and recognizes its other half.

Shutting my eyes, I'm unwilling to see what's there. Call me a fucking coward, but I can't give her what she needs.

Two small hands grip my face. "Come back to me, Aiden. This is our moment. No judgment. No shame. Just you and me, lost in this bliss."

Pressing another kiss to her chest, I kiss my way up to her mouth, unable to resist her big brown eyes. Giving in to the moment, I lose myself in her. Wrapping her long black hair around my fist, I pull back, exposing the sensual column of her neck. Unable to help myself, my tongue peeks out and licks the hollow where her shoulder meets the base of her neck.

Shaking beneath me, Charlotte releases a needy whimper as her hands find their way to my waistband, lowering it and pulling me out. Gasping, her already doe eyes grow even wider as she strokes my entire length from base to tip. "My *god*."

"Don't worry. I promise to go slow at first." Winking, I wrap my right hand around hers, pumping myself one more time before removing her grip.

"Keep doing that, and I'm going to come." Bringing my mouth down onto hers, I smile as I get rid of my sweats.

We're both fully naked. Skin to skin. Flesh to flesh. Souls bared and no fucks to give.

Looking into her eyes, I ask once more, "Are you sure?"

Raising herself, Charlotte's wet slit glides over my cock, her warmth seeking my tip. Bringing my face to hers, Charlotte bites my bottom lip as she impales herself with my cock, her walls gripping my shaft and squeezing.

My eyes roll back in their sockets and I swear I can see God. Holy mother of everything good. Never in my life have I experienced anything so damn good.

My balls tighten and my back tingles, sure signs of an impending orgasm. Needing to take control of this situation before I embarrass myself, I grip her inner thigh, squeeze and open her wide, making sure to hit her sweet spot as I slowly glide out and then back in her delicious cunt.

Charlotte gasps for air and I can see on her face that she feels just as good as I do right now. Wondering if any man has made her feel this good has me seeing red.

Mine.

Pounding into her harder, my body takes on a mind of its own, needing to claim her and mark her as mine.

"Yes. Oh, god. Yes." Panting, Charlotte's nails dig into my back. "Just. Like. That."

"Anything for you, princess." Grunting as I continue to thrust, I bend down into that dip on her neck and suck hard, needing to have as much of her as possible.

Her moan has her arching her back and giving me access to her lower back. Both hands wrap around either side of her small waist, digging my fingers into her supple flesh and bringing her to me with every push of my hips.

Wet skin and muffled grunts have never sounded sweeter. I could spend the rest of my days inside of her and not want for a damn thing more.

A rumble starts in Charlotte's chest before she lets out a long moan. Quickly, I bring my hand to her mouth, trying to quiet her, but Charlotte has other ideas. Taking the edge of my hand, she clamps down and starts to suck through her climax. Milking, sucking, and biting her way through the highest of highs.

The sensation of her mouth on me sends me spiraling into my own release. Unable to hold back any longer as the overwhelming kaleidoscope of emotions washes over me, my dick pulses, releasing ropes of cum into her womb.

In that moment of delirium, she is mine. Burying myself deeper into her, I let my inner cave man out, silently claiming this beautiful woman with every drop I have.

Her eyes open, a multitude of questions swimming through those beautiful orbs. Questions I don't have answers to.

Doing the only thing I know to do, I lower my forehead to hers and ask, "So, will that be a yes, then? Are you coming to the wedding?"

From confused to elated, her broad smile blinds me. "That's most definitely a yes."

Maybe, just maybe, we can find a way to make this work.

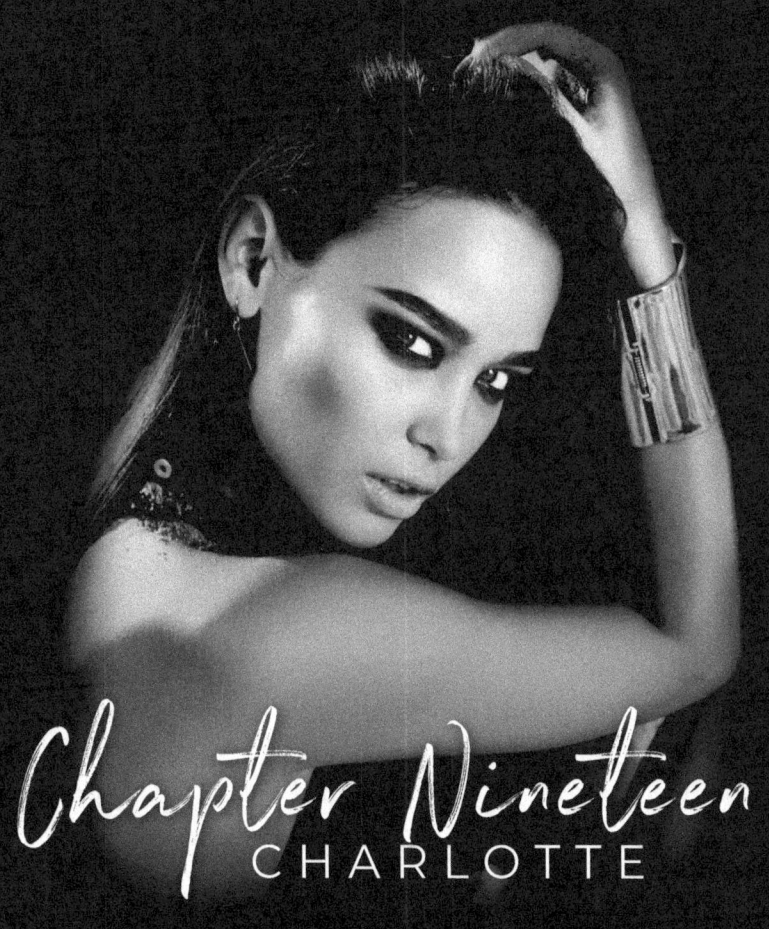

Chapter Nineteen
CHARLOTTE

What have I done?! How could I ever face my sister again, knowing that I've been with a man that was hers in the first place?

The hot water from the shower spray cascades down my body, cleansing away the day's grime but leaving all of the guilt behind.

"Miss Montgomery?" Sylvie calls through the bathroom door, startling me out of my thoughts.

"Yes? Is everything okay?"

"Oh, yes dear. I just wanted to let you know that the dress for tonight's dinner is pressed and on your bed."

"Thank you!" I bury my head back under the spray and groan.

It's been a week since Aiden and I made love. Calling it anything else would be a damn lie. The way he looked at me like I was his world, the tenderness in his touch as he worshiped every inch of me was nothing short of adoration.

What ensued after? The complete opposite.

We fell asleep in each other's arms after I agreed to come with him to the wedding, but when I awoke, he was nowhere to be seen.

Stepping out of my room that morning, it was as if I'd been labeled a leper. He wouldn't even look me in the eye, much less direct a kind word toward me.

Then this morning, William stopped by and demanded Aiden show up to their weekly dinner, and when Aiden tried to use me as an excuse, William shot him right down. Reminding him that his home is one of the safest in the nation and that Bella would love to meet the other woman in the boys' lives.

I smile at the thought. The twins and I have become quite the little team, and I already can't see my life without them.

If only they weren't attached to such an infuriatingly bipolar man.

I get that we aren't the ideal couple. My past, and hell even my present, hold massive obstacles. But couldn't we live in our little bubble just a little while longer?

The water turns ice cold and my breath catches as I quickly turn the knob cutting off the spray. *Time to face reality.*

Wrapping the soft fluffy towel around me, I exit the bathroom and step into my room where a beautiful linen dress sits on the bed.

The squared neckline is structured, a perfect match to the full pleated skirt, hitting just below the knees.

Unable to contain my excitement, I squeal loudly when I see the gorgeous pair of Chanel espadrille wedges sitting to the right of the dress. They aren't even supposed to be out yet. How did they manage to snag a pair?

The door bursts open and a wild-eyed Aiden looks around frantically, gun drawn.

My hands fly to my mouth as I let out another shriek and my towel drops, giving Aiden a full view of my body.

His eyes focus on my naked body and his throat visibly bobs.

"What the—" Titus rushes in and takes inventory as my whole body flushes fifty different shades of red.

"GET OUT!" Aiden roars at Titus, blocking his line of sight as I scurry to pick up the towel laying at my feet.

"Okay, okay. Sheesh. I didn't mean to see your girl naked, man. The screaming—"

"OUT NOW!" Aiden shoves Titus through the door, closing it as soon as his friend is through the threshold. Aiden's head presses into the closed door and he lets out a slow breath. "Why did you scream? You should know that we are all on edge here. You screaming while naked will only invite unwanted eyes."

"You can turn around now, I have the towel back on. And who says they're unwanted." I know he was talking about Titus, but I can't help but poke the bear. He's been ignoring me and this is the most reaction I've gotten from him in the last seven days.

His nostrils flare and his eyes narrow. "Charlotte—"

"What, Aiden? You think you own me because we had one night together? Well, news flash. You don't. Especially if you just throw away what we had like it didn't matter at all."

Three big strides and Aiden has me picked up and pinned against the wall. "I did not throw it away." His deep voice is low as he speaks right into my ear—our cheeks touching, the rough sensation of his stubble against my skin sending shivers down my wet body. His chest vibrates against my own and my legs instinctively wrap around him, needing him closer. "I'm protecting you. That's all I ever do. That's all I ever want."

His words turn my want into full blown rage. How dare he push me away under the guise of protection.

Pushing at his chest, Aiden drops me like a hot potato. All the heat I felt in my lady parts has now traveled to my head and I am fuming. "Protect me? By destroying my heart?" I immediately realize what I've done and grimace.

I've laid my cards out, giving him all the power. He now knows that this is much more than just a fling to me.

His jaw drops and his face goes pale. *Yup. Earth, please swallow me whole.*

Needing to change the subject immediately, I turn to what started this whole mess, "And for your information I wasn't screaming. I was squealing. How in the hell did you manage to snag a pair of the new espadrille wedges? They aren't even out yet!"

Real smooth, Charlotte. Go from heart breaking to superficial in two seconds flat.

Aiden blinks, rightfully confused, so I emphatically point toward the shoes on the bed.

"Oh, um. I called in a favor with Cassie, my daughter's best friend. She's a personal stylist." He walks toward the closet behind him and opens it, revealing a wide selection of casual to formal wear and my jaw practically hits the floor. All of it is designer and all of it is worth a small fortune. "She dropped off all of these things yesterday and Silvie put them all up for you while you were in the shower. You were in there quite a while."

"Aiden," I walk past him and lift a hand to all of the beautiful fabric. "This is too much. I don't even want to imagine what you spent on all this."

"It's not too much. I know you're accustomed to these things and I didn't want you to be without. I've already taken you out of the type of home environment you're used to, the least I could do is give you some of the amenities you enjoy."

Turning toward him, I see his hazel eyes are full of insecurity. *As if I could ever view him as not being enough.*

My hand reaches toward his, squeezing tightly. "This house is much more of a home to me than the estate ever was. You, the boys, and Sylvie..." I stop before I blurt out something I'll regret, like giving him a full blown confession of love and try for something a little less frightening. "You all are like the family I never had, and I wouldn't trade that for anything in the world."

Aiden's tanned skin deepens, his soft smile bringing out that dimple I love so much. "Maybe when this is all over, you can see where we really live." His chest puffs up like a proud peacock, no doubt thinking about that impressive estate of his nestled among five acres, smack dab in the middle of one of the wealthiest neighborhoods in Texas.

I'm about to tell him I'd love that when his proud expression falters and his ice cold walls of indifference are back up, making my heart crumble into a million little pieces right along with it.

"We're leaving in an hour. Please don't be late." Without another glance, he turns and walks out the door, slamming it behind him.

My palms sweat as we approach the massive New England cottage style home. Unable to walk in through the front door for fear of being seen, our blacked-out SUV enters directly into the garage located behind the *porte cochere*. Once inside, the rolling door shuts, leaving us in darkness before the boys pile out excitedly.

"Yessss. We get to use the secret entrance today!"

Secret entrance? Why am I not surprised? Aiden doesn't leave anything to chance, and the option of me being spotted coming or going from one of their residences is not going to happen.

My eyes get used to the dimmed lighting and I see the boys have scurried to the far corner of the garage where there's a pallet on the floor. Aiden pushes a couple of frames on the wall behind him and the pallet rises like something out of a James Bond movie.

Cocking a brow, Aiden waves toward the entrance. "Ladies first."

The boys chuckle as they step aside, "Yes, Char. Ladies first."

Ruffling their hair as I walk past, I can't help but smile. These two have my whole heart. "Okay then, but if I fall you two are going to help me up."

"Yes, ma'am," they both say in unison.

Stepping onto the lowered platform, I pray my wedged heels don't give out. I'm just glad Sylvie didn't come or she'd be forced to come down this ladder to the platform.

Finally down onto the platform, the boys and Aiden join me before we all start to lower deeper into the ground. I'd be lying if I said I wasn't a bit hesitant, the cobwebs around the drop shaft doing little to dispel my fears.

Coming into the light, I see a well maintained corridor, presumably leading into the main home. Okay, this isn't so scary anymore. My shoulders relax and I let out the breath I was holding.

Aiden chuckles beside me, "You okay?"

"Yes." I glare at him. "Not all of us were built for mystery and suspense, you know."

He just smirks at me, placing his hand securely on my lower back as the boys run ahead of us. The feeling of his strong palm pressing against me so intimately sends goose bumps erupting over my skin, and I shudder. Aiden's eyes widen and his mouth goes slack as he realizes what he's done. Just as soon as the intimate gesture arrived it's gone. Aiden drops his hand and the coolness I feel is much more than just the lack of his body's warmth.

Before either of us can say anything, the boys burst through a white door opening into a massive game room. A pool table sits in front of a massive bar area, and directly adjacent to it is a huge television screen surrounded by theatre-style seating.

The twins main line it to the TV and pick up the controllers sitting above one of the many game consoles. The smiles on their faces are priceless and the way they take control over the room lets me know they've spent countless hours in here.

"Boys, you get to play *after* dinner. You know the rules." A beautiful brunette walks into the room and I can't help but stare.

Her piercing gray eyes contrasting with her almost black hair are absolutely stunning, and her round belly does nothing but accentuate the glow in her radiant complexion. She must be eight months along!

Her eyes meet mine and a welcoming smile spreads across her lips. "You must be Charlotte. I'm Bella, Aiden's daughter."

My mouth slacks. I knew Aiden had a daughter, but I just didn't picture a full-grown woman. She's absolutely stunning and my mind wanders to what her mother must've looked like. Shaking my head, I finally snap out of my daze. "Excuse my manners, they seem to have left me. Yes, I'm Charlotte Montgomery." Aiden smirks by my side. Nothing gets past him and the fact that I've chosen to use my maiden name is no exception. "It's so nice to finally meet you. Aiden speaks so highly of you."

"Does he now?" Bella elbows her father as he places one of his big hands on her belly.

"How are you feeling? How's the peanut doing?" He looks at her like she hung the moon, and the love he holds for her is palpable.

"We're both fine. I swear, if I let William dote on me anymore, you'd be seeing me on a literal pedestal. People fanning me and feeding me grapes while I get morbidly obese. The man doesn't even want me walking laps in our gym!"

"Do not exaggerate, woman." William walks in, a playful smile playing at the corner of his lips while a little toddler grips on to his hand.

Crouching down, I meet the little one eye to eye, "And you must be Harper. You are such a beautiful baby."

She babbles something in response and giggles before hiding behind her father.

"She's always a little shy at first, but she will warm to you." Aiden whispers behind me as I rise from my crouched position, his hand finding its way once more to my body, fingers gripping around my waist.

Bella's eyes travel to her father's hand and they widen before quickly glancing at William and smiling. "Let's all head to the dining room. The rest of the crew is already there, and I'm sure they'd love to officially meet you."

Taking in a deep breath, I follow the adorable trio into the rest of their home and brace myself for a night of the unknown.

Once again, I'm left feeling unsure of where I stand or if I even fit in. All I know for certain is that so far, these people feel far more like family than my blood relations ever did, and that's definitely something worth exploring.

Chapter Twenty
CHARLOTTE

"**C**an we finally eat now?" Titus bellows as we enter the room, and a woman who looks an awful lot like William smacks him upside the head.

"Manners." The brunette arches a brow, unfazed by the growl Titus returns in her favor.

William finally steps in, breaking off the visible tension between the two. "Titus, stop staring at my sister like that, and Ashley, hands to yourself, please. We don't need you antagonizing the beast."

"That's right, the beast. Don't you forget it."

"You'd like that wouldn't you." Ashley mumbles under her breath and I can't help but chuckle. Wrong move. This brings all eyes back to me and I squirm under their gaze.

"Charlotte, please sit." Bella pulls a chair and I do as asked.

Aiden sits next to me as the introductions around the table begin. "You've already met my daughter Bella and her fiancé William. He motions to them with his hand, then of course there's Titus." His jaw clenches and his hand balls into a fist. Meanwhile, my face turns red as everyone glances at each other, wondering what the hell brought on this moment of tension. But Aiden clears his throat and continues before anyone can get their two cents in. "Then here we have Ashely, William's sister, who lives in Florida but spends a lot of time with Bella and helping out with Harper."

Speaking of, I see a blond woman resembling a Viking setting up a highchair next to Bella. I see William gingerly plop his little girl down into the chair as the woman scoots it forward to the table so she has her very own place setting.

At the sight, my ovaries clench and my eyes glisten. I can't help but feel the twinge of jealousy, wondering if I'll ever get the chance to have a family of my very own.

"And these are Ren and Cassie, they—"

"Oh, Cassie! Thank you so very much for picking out all of the amazing clothes that now line my closet. I can't believe the connection you have with some of these designers!" Everyone laughs and my cheeks burn, as I realize I've just cut off Aiden—something no one ever does—to gush about clothing.

"I know. I'm chopped liver compared to what my Cassie can bring to the table." The man sitting next to her, presumably Ren, places a kiss to Cassie's temple and she blushes.

"Stop. You know you're the real catch here." She looks up at him with such adoration in her eyes. These two couldn't be more adorable if they tried.

"Gag me now..." A man to the right of Cassie makes a gagging motion and the girl next to him giggles. She looks to be in her late teens.

Aiden sighs before motioning toward the man, "*This* is Hudson and sitting next to him is his little sister, Alyssa."

The pair visibly flinch at that label, and my first thought is that there must be something more to their story.

"And last, but certainly not least, there is Chef. Her name is Margerie, but she likes to go by Chef. This Michelin Star rated woman gets to call herself whatever she wants and we will all gladly obey, as long as we get some of her amazing cooking." Aiden smiles and the laughs around the table let me know he's definitely not kidding.

"Now can we eat?" Titus looks at Ashley like he's asking for permission and I can't help but giggle. This man is one of the most domineering, testosterone-filled males I've ever met. Yet here he is, looking like a little boy asking for his cookies before dinner.

As if on cue, Chef lifts two massive silver domes revealing the entrees underneath. A succulent roast in one dish and a salmon covered in a cream and caper sauce in the other. My mouth waters and my stomach grumbles at the feast before me and I can't help but whisper, "Yes, please."

Aiden smiles as his hand reaches underneath the table, grabbing hold of my thigh and squeezes. "Just wait until you see her dessert."

Suddenly I forget all about the food and my thoughts go straight to the way his grip felt on my thigh as he spread me open. Aiden's eyes drop to my mouth, the tip of his tongue peeking out and wetting his bottom lip.

"Someone serve the food quickly, before these two devour each other in front of the kids." Hudson teases, but Aiden isn't having any of it. He swiftly kicks Hudson under the table, his glare searing into the other man's scalp as he doubles over in pain.

"*Oomph.* I was only kidding, man." Hudson shakes his head, before murmuring, "*Kind of.*"

Either Aiden doesn't hear or he chooses to ignore the comment. Either way, the food is getting served and I'm too hungry to care as I dive into a bite of the juiciest chicken I've ever tasted. "Chef, I'll call you my queen if I can get another serving of this!" I smile up at her as soon as I've finished my first bite.

"Well, dear. You are welcome to my cooking anytime." She winks at me before continuing, her eyes locking on Aiden. "I have a feeling I'll be seeing a lot more of you."

My cheeks flush for the millionth time today—I've completely lost track—and the only thing I know is that despite my apprehensions about this dinner, this is the most fun I've had in awhile.

With my clothes on, that is.

Aiden

"What do you mean ransacked?!" My voice is unrecognizable even to myself. "Is Sylvie okay?"

"Yes, she was out running errands when we noticed one of our men was missing. We believe it to be an inside job and he was the one who ransacked the home while Sylvie was out." Jimmy lets me in on the details of what transpired at the safe house while we all sat around William's table and ate, oblivious to the destruction going on back home.

Home. That isn't our home, but fuck if Charlotte hasn't made it feel like one.

Charlotte. She's going to be distraught when I tell her the news, but there's no way we could stay there now.

"You there, boss?" Jimmy's voice brings me back to business.

"Yes. Do our usual sweep and send a team in search of our man. We need answers."

"Yes. We'll report as soon as we have something."

The phone cuts out just as Charlotte steps into the hallway.

"Everything okay? I could hear you all the way in the game room." She approaches me hesitantly, as if she were afraid I'd detonate any moment.

Poor woman has been conditioned to walk on eggshells. "Come here." I open my arms wide and bring her into my chest, placing a kiss on top of her head. "What I have to tell you won't be pleasant. Do you want the good news or the bad news first?"

"Good news." Charlotte buries her head into my chest, tightening her hold around me.

"Preston has been served with the divorce papers."

Gasping, Charlotte looks up into my eyes with so much hope, I'm almost hesitant to tell her the rest.

"That's great news! Right?" The realization that there's bad news to share has her smile sinking into a sad frown and I can't help but bring both of my hands to her face, cradling her as if she were the most precious crystal—because let's face it, to me she *is*.

"We aren't sure if this is Preston's doing, but the house was ransacked earlier."

Her beautiful face contorts into one experiencing excruciating pain. "Oh my god! Sylvie! Did they hurt her?"

This beautiful soul, her sanctuary was demolished and her first thought goes to a person, not things. She couldn't be more different from Clara if she tried.

"Sylvie is fine. Thankfully, she was out running errands while this happened. Like I said, we aren't sure if this is Preston's doing. His secretary Mikaela accepted service of the divorce petition but we've yet to receive a response as to how he's wanting to proceed." I lower my hands to her waist and squeeze, trying to impart as much strength into my touch as possible without hurting her. "I'm here. Everything is going to be okay. If this situation at the safe house was Preston, then we'll handle it. I give you my word."

"Your word." Charlotte's brow lifts right along with the corner of her mouth. "I seem to be collecting a lot of those lately. I'm quite the lucky girl."

"You're not going to feel too lucky when I tell you the rest of the plan..."

Squeezing her eyes shut, she takes in a deep breath before asking, "What's the plan now?"

"We can't go back to the safe house now that it's been compromised, and I definitely don't want to be driving around with you where you could probably be spotted. So..." I tilt her chin up, looking into her big brown eyes. "We are staying here."

"We're what?!"

"Staying here. The boys already have their rooms here on the second floor, right next to Harper's and we can stay in the guest room. It's just down the hall and on the first floor."

Charlotte's entire face flushes bright red, and I realize what I've just insinuated. Quickly trying to do damage control, I add, "You'll take the bed and I'll take the couch, of course. This home only has five rooms, and I didn't want to bunk with the boys on the second floor while you are on the first. Safety measures and all."

Her eyes narrow, probably calling me on my bullshit. The truth is William is on this floor and this place is locked up tighter than Fort Knox. Still. Nobody could protect her like I would.

Before I can try to justify it any further, Charlotte concedes. "Okay."

"Okay?" My mouth slacks ajar as I openly gape at her. This was way too easy.

"Did I stutter?" She purses her lips to the side before continuing. "Good thing you don't snore." With a wink, this little vixen turns, escaping my arms and leaving me wanting more. *Lord, I'm in trouble.*

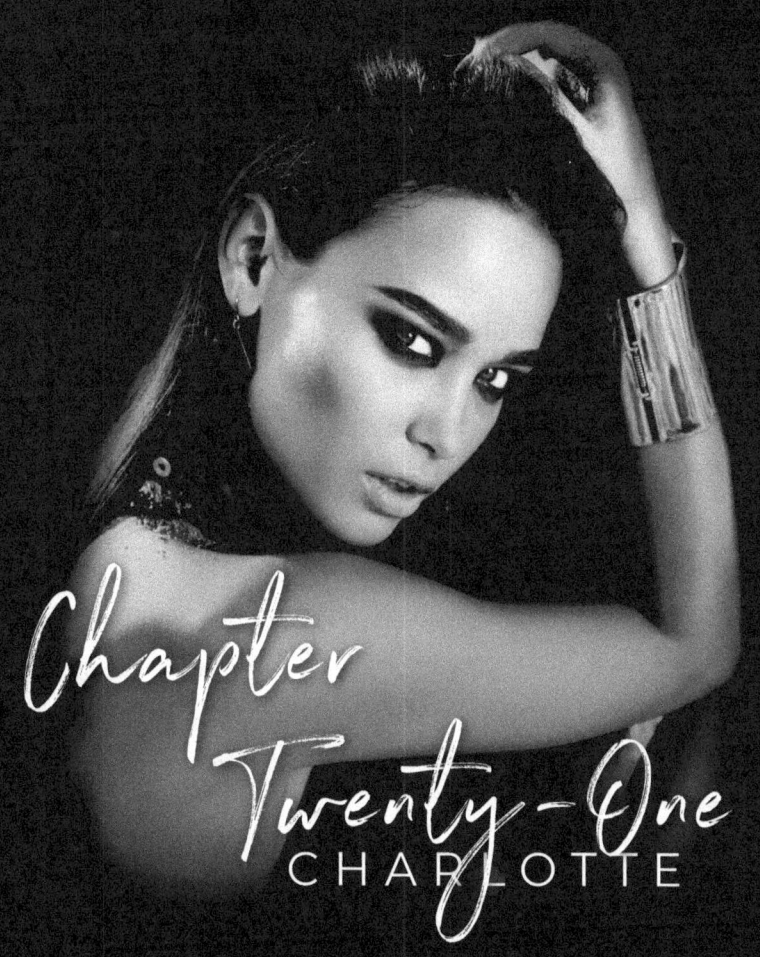

Chapter Twenty-One

CHARLOTTE

Act cool. Just keep walking. Don't look back.

Oh. My. God. I need a moment to compose myself. Sliding into the powder room, I close the door and press my forehead against the cool slab of wood.

Instead of worrying about the state of our home, I'm over here stressing about spending the night with Aiden. Yes, we've slept together before, but this is different. He'll be staying the whole night and everyone will know about it.

It's already hard enough for me to keep myself in check, now add in the pressure of everyone wondering what's going on behind closed doors and I'm about to combust!

A knock on the door startles me, sending me flying back and falling onto the toilet. Thank god the lid was down or my soaked bottom could've been super awkward to explain.

"Yes? Almost done."

"Char, it's Bella. Can I have a word?"

Quickly scurrying off the seat, I make my way to the door and pry it open. Bella's hesitant smile shines back at me, melting away some of my nerves.

Stepping out into the hallway, she motions me down the hall. I'm about to ask her where we're headed when she opens a door off the corridor. The room is beautifully decorated in pale gray and soft pink. There's a massive four poster bed, and across it a chaise adjacent to a large bay window.

"This is where you'll be staying with Dad. Please let me know if you need anything." Bella opens her arms wide, showcasing the room. "There's also an attached bath so you don't have to worry about roaming down the hallway in the middle of the night and you already know where the kitchen is in case you need anything."

My face must be the color of a stop light by now. I can't believe she's talking to me so casually about shacking up with her father. Granted, he said he would take the couch, but how does she know that?

"Thank you, Bella. I really appreciate your help during this trying time. My life isn't usually this full of drama." My gaze falls to the floor, unable to look her in the eye. She must think I'm a hot mess and probably doesn't want me anywhere near her father.

"Please sit." Bella lowers herself onto the chaise, patting the spot next to her.

My palms sweat and stomach churns as I do as asked, all while still avoiding her gaze.

"I'll just cut to the chase. I'm sure you have a lot going on with the senator, your divorce, and now whatever's happened at the safe house."

Finally looking at her, I open my mouth to say something but she stops me, placing one hand up in the air and shaking her head.

"Please, let me finish. I know you have your own stuff going on, but I want to make sure that it doesn't drag my father down with it. I'm not sure what you two have going on, but it's safe to say that I've never seen my father act like this toward a woman. Not even my mother." She sighs out a breath, her brows furrowing. "I'm not saying you aren't a wonderful person, all I'm saying is that my dad has been through a lot and having someone play with his heart will only set back all of the amazing progress—"

Needing to interject, I grab her hand and squeeze it gently. "I've loved your father for as long as I can remember. You might not know me, but I know him and I would never do anything to hurt him. This might be a little TMI, but I have a feeling you'll understand." It's my turn to let out a shaky breath, unsure if I should be divulging as much as I'm about to. "Aiden was always the forbidden older man in my life. The one too far out of reach for me to even dare dream of. And to be honest, I'm not sure of what's going on between us either. But I do know that if I'm ever given a chance to hold his heart with mine, then I wouldn't do anything to lose it. I'd cherish it and appreciate it for what it is, a gift."

Bella's eyes glisten in the dim lighting and my heart clenches, waiting for her response.

"You have no idea how much that means to me." She squeezes my hand before pulling me toward her for an embrace.

"Here you both—" Aiden walks into what I could only assume is a very curious scene. "Everything okay here?"

Releasing each other, we both turn to Aiden with wet eyes and sappy smiles. "Everything is fine, Daddy." Bella tries to get up but needs a little push from me, her belly throwing off her center of gravity and all. "Now if you two will excuse me, I need to go get Harper ready for bedtime." She kisses Aiden on the cheek before closing the door behind her, and I swear I think I see her wink at me.

Aiden clears his throat as he lowers himself onto the spot Bella just vacated, his broad hand reaching for my back and rubbing slow circles. "You okay?"

"Yes." My whole body warms at the concern in his typically callous eyes. "We were just having some girl talk. I like Bella a lot. You did good." My hand falls to his thigh and I sense him tense up on me.

"No. I didn't. That's all her. She was just born amazing. Honestly, I'm lucky I didn't fuck her up completely."

"Stop." My hand tries to squeeze his thigh, but it's so wide I barely manage to apply any pressure. "Last time I checked, you're human. It's not easy being a parent, and a single one at that. Look, I'm not making excuses for you, but now that Bella is a mother to Harper, I'm sure she understands. There is no manual on how to be the perfect parent and all we can do is try our best, putting in as much love and patience as we are able."

Aiden stares at me, jaw clenched and narrowed eyes, before his hand reaches out, wrapping behind my nape and bringing me to him. Our lips crash into one another's, finding their other half as they bite, nip, and suck.

Home. That's what he is.

Wherever I go, whatever I do, he'll always be my home.

Taking his lower lip into my mouth, I lick and suck, eagerly wanting more. Aiden lowers me down onto the chaise and I open my legs wide, wrapping them around his waist. As soon as his hardened length hits my center, I moan, writhing underneath him and pressing myself into him with the help of my heels on his ass.

"My *principessa perfetta*. I can't stay away." His pained face looks down at me, and I can see the struggle in his eyes.

Reaching up to his face, I bring him down to me. "Then don't. Stop thinking and just feel." I gently rub my lips against his, back and forth. "Doesn't this feel good?"

"You know it does." He thrust his hips forward, his ridge hitting my clit in just the right spot, causing another moan to escape.

A hard knock on the door has me sucking in my panting breath and looking up at Aiden. Our bubble has burst once more and even though I'm a lady, I could definitely punch whoever knocked on the door just now.

Aiden lowers his mouth to mine, pressing a chaste kiss to my lips before getting up and adjusting himself. "Anyone ever tell you you're adorable when you pout?"

I scoff as I sit up, "I'm most definitely not pouting."

"Sure thing, princess." Aiden opens the door slightly, enough to let me see the outline of William's head.

"We got our man."

Those four words have Aiden's entire posture going rigid. "Alright."

Without another word or even a glance back, Aiden exits the room, leaving me cold and in the dark once again.

Aiden

There's only one thing replaying in my mind over and over. *Protect Charlotte at all costs.*

Following William into his office, I see that the other men are already here.

"Took you long enough," Ren grumbles, but the smirk on his lips lets me know he's teasing.

William sucks in air with pursed lips, "Yeah, it sounded pretty intense in there. I didn't want to interrupt, but I knew I needed to get to you before things got too heavy. We have business to attend to."

"You were fucking listening in on me and Charlotte?!" I see red, the only mission is to protect her virtue and this sure as shit isn't doing that.

"Wow, chill out *Dad*." William tries to push me off of him and it's just then I realize I have his shirt in a tight grip. "This is family and we don't rat on each other. You should know that by now."

"Give him a break," Titus chimes in. "You would've been the same way had someone been listening in on you and Bella. Don't go acting like you and Ren aren't psycho overprotective over your women."

Now I turn to Titus, practically growling, "Charlotte is not my woman."

"You keep telling yourself that, brother." Ren shakes his head as he chuckles. "We all see it as clear as day, but you keep living on that river called *de Nile*."

"Enough. It's time we cut to business." Hudson cuts into the banter, his brows dropped and mouth formed into a thin line. Something's up with him. He's usually the jokester, ribbing everyone and making us all lovingly miserable.

"You okay?" The space between my eyes crinkles as I frown.

"He's just butt hurt because he has to babysit his stepsister. Didn't you hear? She's shacking up with big bro over here." Titus rolls in his lips, biting back a laugh.

"Shut your pie hole, Titus." Hudson throws a wadded napkin at Titus' head. "I'm just wanting to get to the issue at hand. I'd think lover boy here would want to know since it's regarding the incident that happened at the safe house."

All eyes fall on me, and I choose to ignore the stupid remark for the sake of efficiency, "Talk to me. What do we know?"

"Our guy was found at the Arkansas border." William's tone is cautious and I know there's more to the story.

"*And.*"

"The other men were transporting him back to our SUV when a sniper took him out."

"Are you fucking kidding me?! Did anyone get any information out of him before they took him out?"

"Nope." Titus pops the 'p' before continuing. "All we know is that he is the one who ransacked the home and that he admitted to messing up. We don't know why he did it or who ordered it, if anyone."

I roll my eyes. "Someone definitely ordered it, or else there wouldn't have been a sniper."

"I'm just playing Devil's advocate. Don't shoot the messenger." Titus raises his hands as he chuckles. "Get it? Shoot the messenger?"

Shaking my head, I close my eyes. "Man. That's tasteless, even for you." Rubbing my hand across my face, I start thinking of the next steps. "Okay. We need to get a hold of his phone records and any surveillance video of him we can get our hands on. There's gotta be a clue linking him to the person who placed the order."

"He knew your schedule, so he definitely didn't want anyone home while he did it." Ren rubs his chin, voicing my exact thoughts. "Now, if we could figure out what he was searching for or who sent him."

I rub at the back of my neck as my head falls back. "My bet is on Preston, but what could he be looking for?"

"Did Charlotte take anything from the house?" William asks.

"The only thing I took was her go bag. She had it ready to go, but there wasn't anything in it other than clothing and toiletries."

"Well, it's not the evidence we have on him. He knows that it's safely stored in the cloud, and it's definitely not Charlotte's tampons. So..."

I glare at Hudson, "Crass much? The sooner we get ahold of his phone records and question the rest of the team, the sooner we'll have answers. One of the other men must've noticed something off about our rat. Where's the team now?"

Titus answers, "They're taking Sylvie to the airport. Per your orders, she'll be staying with her daughter until this all blows over. Once the drop-off is made, they're heading to HQ and awaiting your orders."

"Good. I'll want to interrogate them personally. William, will you stay here with Charlotte?"

"You know it. I don't plan on venturing far from home for the next week. We are seven days out from the wedding, Bella will lose her shit if something happens to this mug of mine before then." Rubbing his jaw, the fool grins.

I shake my head, choosing to ignore the invitation for a jab. "Alright, Casanova. I'll be back as soon as possible. In the meantime, you three dig into phone records and any possible surveillance. Let me know if anything comes up."

"Ten-four, lover boy." Titus smirks, batting his lashes in imitation of a love struck fool.

I flip them off as I exit William's office, mumbling, "Assholes. All of you."

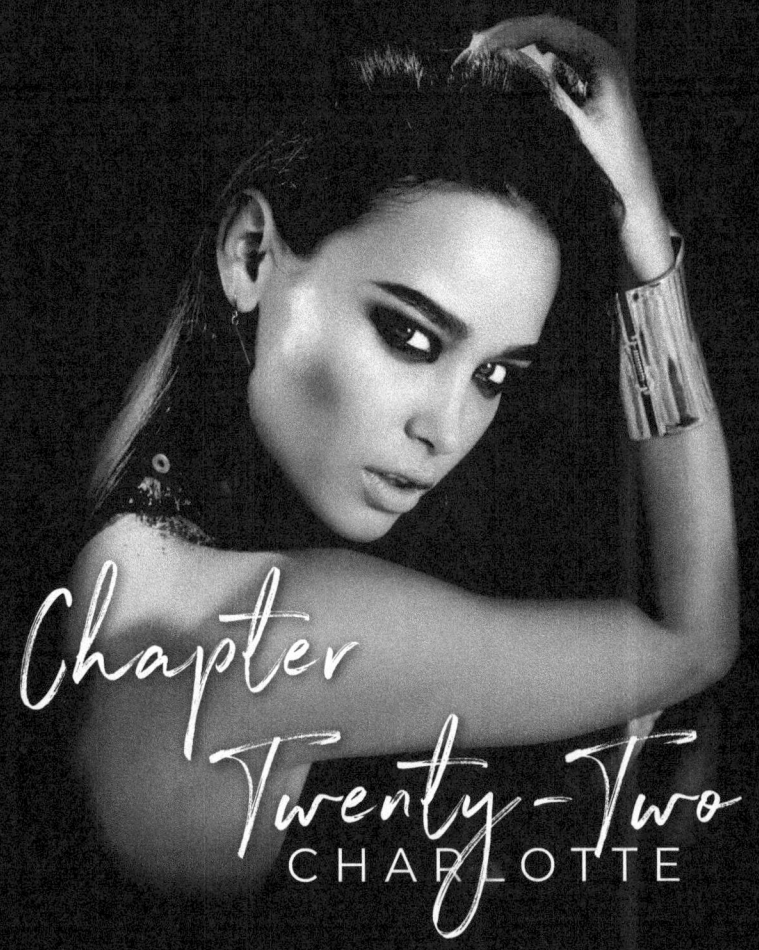

Chapter
Twenty-Two
CHARLOTTE

I'm tossing and turning for the fifteen millionth time. I've gotten no sleep tonight. The clock on the nightstand indicates it's about to be five in the morning and there's still no sign of Aiden.

He left without so much as a backward glance. I'm sure it was about whoever ransacked the safe house, but he could have at least given me a heads-up that I'd be alone all night.

I'm about to roll over again when I hear the door creek open. I can see Aiden's tall frame pause at the foot of the bed before laying down on the minuscule chaise.

There's no way he thinks he can sleep on that thing comfortably.

Looking up, I can't help but laugh. "Are you really going to try to fit yourself into that?"

"Yes." That one word sends goose bumps rising across my skin.

"Come on. You and I both know that there's no way you'll be able to sleep on it comfortably." I lick my lips, anticipating his refusal but hoping for his acceptance. "I have a king-size bed. There's plenty of room for you. We wouldn't even have to touch if you don't want."

He groans against the arm raised over his face. "You know I want. That's the problem."

"It's not a problem if you don't make it one. Like I said, you can stay on your side and I'll stay on mine."

I'm thinking there will have to be another round of verbal sparring before he agrees to anything, but to my shock, he lifts himself off of the small piece of furniture and makes it to the opposite side of the bed.

"Fine, but you keep those luscious lips of yours all the way over there." His brows raise while he points to the other edge of the bed. "I'm not responsible for my actions if you come any closer."

Biting my lip, I scooch to the edge, not wanting to spook the man back onto the chaise. "Whatever you say, boss."

The bed dips and my breath halts. My stomach flutters like it did the first time I laid eyes on this man. Since that first instance, he's ingrained himself into the very fiber of my being. It's as if my body calls to his, needing its other half to become a whole.

Rolling to my side, I give him my back. If I face him any longer, I'm liable to jump him. Shutting my eyes, I try to force myself to sleep, but it never comes. Instead, I feel movement behind me, the rustle of the sheets sending my heartbeat spiking.

"We found a possible link to Preston and the man who ransacked the safe house." His deep voice has me turning quickly, slamming directly into his broad chest. Instinctively, his arms wrap around me, his lips falling to my forehead. "It's okay, *principessa.* I won't let him hurt you. You're safe."

My leg hitches over his and I feel him press into me as he groans.

"Baby, I don't think this is a good idea. I should go back to the chaise."

"Please, Aiden. Don't leave me." My brown eyes meet his hazel, and a million words are spoken all at once. I don't see myself as a weak woman, and I've never been one to beg, but for this man I'd crawl across broken glass.

Aiden cups my face, tilting it toward his and bringing his lips gently down onto mine. "I could never deny you anything." He whispers into my mouth, softly stroking my cheek with his thumb. "But if I stay in this bed, the only thing going on will be sleep." I pout and he nips at my lower lip. "Get some sleep, beautiful. The girls have a full day for you tomorrow. From what I hear, they've dragged you into wedding planning."

Resting my head on his chest, I burrow deeper into him, loving the sense of calm and safety he brings. *My home.*

Listening to the steady beat of his heart, I let myself fall— deep into sleep, deep into safety, and deep into love.

Aiden

Heaven. That's where I must be.

My hand cups Charlotte's breast, my thumb flicking her hardened nipple as she undulates her ass against my aching cock. Rocking it into the ridge of her ass, I groan, practically ready to come all over her creamy skin. The satin of her nightgown has ridden up, exposing her backside and the tiny slip of satin covering her round bottom.

This is the most vivid dream I've had of her, and I don't want to wake up.

Nipping at her ear, I take the tiny lobe into my mouth, sucking while I roll her nipple between my thumb and forefinger.

Her little hand reaches behind, lowering my boxers and taking me out.

"Fuck, baby. I'm about to come and I'm not even inside you."

"I can fix that." She turns, the satin strap of her nightgown falling and exposing the most beautiful breasts I've ever seen. Unable to help myself, my mouth finds her dusky pink nipple, licking and suckling before she pulls away with a moan.

Charlotte kisses her way down my chest, her hands running along my sides until she reaches the base of my dick. Looking up at me with those big brown eyes, she grins like the cat that ate the canary. "Mine." She kisses the tip before licking the bead of pre-cum off.

Cupping her face with both hands, I whisper, "Yours."

She ends the torture, finally taking me into her mouth, swallowing me all the way to the base. "Fuuuuuuck." I roar as my head falls back, eyes rolling right along with it.

She hums as she eases me in and out of her talented mouth, and I feel my balls tighten with the impending release. Needing to finish inside her, I reach down, lifting her and flipping her so she's beneath me.

My hands fall down her curves, reveling in the softness of her skin. I reach for her panties and rip them off with one swift pull. Her gasp makes me grin, "Mine."

She gives me a salacious smile as she takes my hand, bringing it to her mound. "Yours."

Three fingers slide inside her warm pussy—wet and slick, ready for my entry. Her body arches, raising her breasts and bringing them within reach of my greedy mouth, drooling with the need to taste them.

Taking one into my mouth, I apply pressure and roll the nub between my teeth, all while pumping in and out of her tight walls.

She begins to contract around my fingers, letting me know she's about to come.

The sight of her, writhing in ecstasy makes me envious of my own damn hand. I want to own every part of her, fill every crevice of her pleasure and claim her as mine.

Taking my fingers out, she whimpers. "What? Why?"

Her confused expression is adorable and I can't help but chuckle as I stroke myself.

"Because I need you, baby." Taking the head of my cock I flick at the bundle of nerves between her folds, and I'm rewarded with the most delicious moan.

"Aiden, please. Fuck me."

Such dirty words from such a proper mouth.

Her words have my cock pulsing in my hand, needing to find its way home.

Unable to hold back any longer, I line myself up and slam home, pumping twice before she's squeezing my cock so hard we're both exploding into the most insane climax of my life. Her walls continue to pulse around me, milking my release for what feels like an eternity.

I can stay here, inside her forever.

Bringing my lips down to hers, I kiss her softly while my seed fills her, marking her as mine. "You're perfect, *principessa*. So damn perfect."

Her legs are wrapped around my hips, her heels pressed into my ass and pushing me deeper. "I—"

Her sweet voice is cut off by the vibration of my phone on the nightstand. My eyes fall to the flashing light and then the woman beneath me.

This isn't a dream.

The memories of me slipping into bed with Charlotte slam into me like a sledgehammer to the chest. We fell asleep in each other's arms. What kind of idiot doesn't know that this would inevitably happen?

Our attraction is otherworldly. I've never experienced this overwhelming need before, and my ass should have known better.

"Aiden, are you okay?" Charlotte's big brown eyes look up at me, concern riddled all over her beautiful face.

The last thing I want is to upset her. She's been through so much and I don't need to add to that. Kissing the tip of her nose, I finally slide out of her. The cold air hitting me and serving as a cold reminder that I didn't even think of using protection.

"Shit, Char. I didn't use a condom."

Her face flushes as she lifts herself on her forearms. "We didn't use one last time either."

I run my hand over my face while letting out a shaky breath. I've even chastised myself about this very thing with her. "Damn, I'm sorry, baby."

"It's okay. I've only ever been with one other man, and I don't think I'm ovulating."

This news has me wanting to rip my hair out. A mixture of rage, jealousy and self-loathing washes over me, unable to breathe in my own skin. "Well, I'm clean."

Reaching over to the nightstand, I see that it was a message from Preston's office. They want to meet up with Charlotte to discuss the divorce. Why they're contacting me instead of her lawyer is worrisome. What the hell are they trying to imply?

"Aiden," Charlotte's shaky voice has me looking up from my phone. "Are you mad at me?"

Damn, I didn't mean to make her feel bad. Wrapping her up in my arms, I kiss her forehead gently. "No, Char. You're perfect. So damn perfect." Pulling back, I look into her eyes. "I'm just mad at the situation. No matter what I say or do, we always end up back here, in each other's arms. So why fight it? At least while we're within these four walls. Hell, my family already sees us as being together."

She bites her lip, holding back a grin. "I like that idea. I like it a lot."

Capturing her mouth in one last kiss, I finally rip myself away, getting out of the bed. "Mine." I wink at her before heading into the shower, needing to get my head on straight.

I'm a greedy man, wanting to steal away what's not rightfully mine. But now that I've had her, I'll be damned if I let anyone take her away from me.

Come at me with all you have, Preston. I'll fight you to the death for this woman.

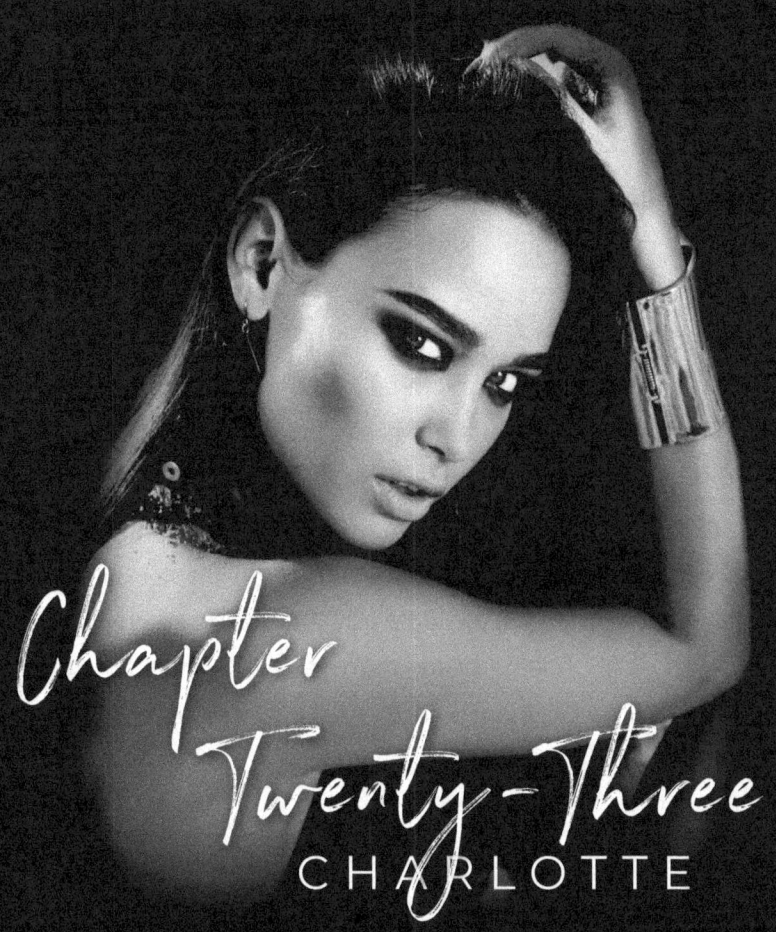

Chapter Twenty-Three

CHARLOTTE

"Mimosas!" The one named Cassie dances as she moves around the living area with a bottle of Champaign. "Well, except for the bride. She gets *virgin* mimosas." Blowing Bella a kiss, she giggles.

"Morning everyone." I walk in, hesitant to join in on their fun.

"Charlotte!" Bella waddles toward me. "I swear. I wanted to put the wedding off until after the baby, but William was adamant about all of us having the same last name when Alexander arrives." Grabbing hold of my arm, she pulls me toward the center of the room, depositing me down into a cream sofa.

Ashley plops down next to me, apparently already having downed most of her drink. "You got here just in time. Cassie brought over the bridesmaid dresses, and although you're not officially in the wedding, she brought you a couple of dresses in the same color scheme as the rest of us."

My chest squeezes and my face flushes. The inclusion these ladies are offering me is something I've never experienced before. Not in my family, and certainly not in the stuffy social circles I'm accustomed to. I smile, turning toward Cassie, "Thank you. I hope it wasn't too much trouble."

"None whatsoever. Aiden had already given me your sizes, so it was no big deal to pull a couple of extra dresses." She hands me a flute full of the bubbly drink and winks. "Besides, he gave me his black charge card and told me to go wild shopping for you. How could I say no to that?"

Now *I know* my cheeks are blazing red. Taking a sip of my drink, I choose to plead the fifth in regard to Aiden. Especially in front of his daughter.

"Oh, stop. Can't you see she's bashful?" Ashley chastises Cassie, but she just brushes her off.

"She needs to get used to us. Now that she's part of the fam-bam she'll be seeing a lot of us and you know there are no secrets between the ladies of WRATH."

Hudson's little stepsister, Alyssa, spits into her glass while Bella pats her back. "You okay, sweetie?"

"She probably freaked out about the secret thing, didn't you doll? It's okay, I meant between us. We keep plenty of secrets from the men." She cackles as she throws back some more of her drink. "Don't worry. We won't be telling Hudson we let you drink.

If I didn't know any better, I'd say he's taken on this overprotective role a little too seriously."

"A little too seriously is putting it mildly," Ashley mumbles into her drink, but she doesn't comment any further.

"Okay, let's get down to business. We have a couple of things to go through, but just as an FYI, we are adding you to our spa appointments later in the week." Cassie points at me before continuing. "For now, we have to finalize the guest list and table settings."

"Oh, I want Charlotte at the head table with us." Bella purses her lips, trying to bite back a full grin. "If the sounds coming out of your room this morning are any indication, it won't be long before all of us are sitting at your head table."

That's it. Earth, swallow me whole please. *I. Am. Mortified.*

Ashley grabs my hand and squeezes. "It's part of the hazing process. They're like sharks, these ones. If you show them a drop of blood, they'll be out for more." Patting my hand, she attempts to temper my embarrassment. "Best to remain stoic, not show them any emotion."

"Is that what you think you do?" Bella shoots Ashley a megawatt grin. "Don't think we aren't on to you and that not-so-mystery man of yours."

"I thought there were no secrets?" Alyssa asks innocently.

"That's right. So why don't you fess up already. It's not as if we don't already know what's up." Cassie raises a brow, staring down poor Ashley.

"Well, it's not a secret if you claim to already know, is it?" Ashley spits back with a cock of her own brow.

"But it's not as fun if it doesn't come from you." Cassie pouts as she rolls out a rack full of beautiful dresses. They're all a beautiful pale shade of pink. They have a fitted corset that's ruched with delicate organza and cuts off at the waist before flowing down into the most beautiful skirt.

Cassie pulls a dress off the rack and walks it to me. "This is my first pick for you! Aiden's jaw will drop as soon as he sees you in it."

"Oh, we're not together." My face heats for the fifty millionth time today as I try to brush off what they must all be thinking. "He's my sister's ex-boyfriend. We just go way back, but there's nothing there romantically."

"Sure thing, darling. That moaning we all heard must have been you playing porno on the television." Cassie purses her lips as her brows lift. "Just so you know, your room butts right against this one and y'all weren't exactly trying to be quiet."

Okay, I'm full-on hyperventilating at this point. Aiden's daughter is sitting right across from me and I can't bear to look at her directly.

"Oh my god, I'm going to pee myself if you don't stop making me laugh!" Bella squeaks out between full bellied laughs. "I see that you're horrified at the idea of being heard, but years with Cassie has chiseled away at whatever sexual waspiness I once possessed."

"I'm not sure waspiness is a word." Alyssa's brows furrow and the sight is enough to break me out of whatever shame I was feeling. This conversation is just too awkwardly funny, I can't help but giggle, the other women following suit.

"You get the picture," Bella finally manages to get out, dabbing at the corner of her eyes. "But seriously, no secrets and no shame here. Ever."

Raising my glass, I toast, "Well, it seems like all of my laundry has been aired out. So cheers to that!"

"Cheers!" Our glasses raised and our hearts warmed, I think I've found a new family in these ladies and I love it.

Aiden

By the time I make it back to the house, it's well past noon. Searching out the women, I find them all in the media room.

The boys are playing video games meanwhile the women are cooing over Harper and her princess dress.

"Hey, Daddy." Bella beams up at me as she twirls Harper. "Isn't her flower girl dress too stinkin' cute?!"

"She really is adorable, sweetie." A vision of Charlotte holding a little girl of our own flashes before me and my breathing picks up. Thanks to my carelessness, that could very well be a possibility.

"You okay?" Charlotte's furrowed brows are aimed right at me, concern riddling her face.

The fact that she is so in tune with me, that she catches the slight shift in my breathing, is telling. We really are connected. "Yes, I'm fine. Though I do need to talk to you about something when you get a chance."

ELEANOR ALDRICK

All the women glance back and forth between themselves, and I wonder what they've been talking about while I've been gone.

"Sure. Is there any news?" Charlotte rises from her place between Bella and Ashley, hesitantly making her way toward me.

"Yes." As soon as we've stepped out into the hallway, I let her in on my concerns. "I'm not sure if you've checked your email today, but Preston's counsel sent out a letter directed to me but listed you in the CC."

"No, I haven't checked. I've been so caught up with the ladies today that I haven't had a chance to deal with any of that." She blows out a breath as she rolls her eyes. "Let me guess, he's not agreeing to an uncontested divorce."

I snort at the idea that Preston would willingly let her go without a fight. "That man doesn't know the meaning of the word uncontested. He'd fight his own shadow if he thought it didn't kiss his ass enough."

"You're definitely right about that." Raising a brow, she shakes her head. "So what did the email say?"

Pushing the door open to her room, I take her hand and walk her to the chaise. I'm glad she didn't let me sleep on this thing. We barely fit sitting down.

"He wants to negotiate the terms, see if you can come to some sort of agreement."

She chews on her bottom lip and I have the urge to pluck it from her teeth, soothing the bruised areas with my tongue.

"I don't know if seeing him is such a good idea. Can't we negotiate through our attorneys, and why wasn't Thompson the one they emailed instead of me?"

186

"Those are very good questions. I think they were trying to send a message, implying that you and I have something going on, maybe possibly give him the upper hand somehow." Her cheeks flush with that beautiful rose color, making me reach out and pull her into an embrace. "Don't worry, they have no basis to use that against you. Your petition was filed under the grounds of insupportability and you didn't have a prenup. As long as you remain adamant that there is no hope of reconciliation, then you don't have to worry about him trying to use a possible relationship against you."

"I don't know Aiden. Even if it won't give him the legal upper hand, he's a vindictive man. He'd find a way to use it somehow."

"Well, if he wants to play dirty then we can air out his dirty laundry, letting the courts see exactly what type of man he is."

Her body stills as she chews on the inside of her cheek. "So tell me again why we have to meet in person?"

"You don't have to if you don't want to. Especially with your history together. If you choose to meet in person, then I will be there with you along with Thompson." I raise my hand, rubbing slow circles on her back, trying to impart as much comfort as possible through my touch. "But you know that sooner or later you'll have to see him. Just know that whatever happens, I'll be there by your side."

Her glassy eyes blink, a single tear falling down her rosy cheek. "Aiden, I—" her voice trembles and I'm overcome with the need to hold her.

Pulling her into my chest, I whisper against her hair. "Shhh. It's all going to be okay. We will get through this. You've always been a fighter, Charlotte. This is no different."

Her face tilts toward mine, her breath mingling with mine and drawing me in. I press my lips to hers in a slow and sensual kiss.

Her mouth parts and my tongue glides across her lips before entering its home.

"You lovebirds done in there? Dinner is ready." William's knocking on the door breaks our kiss and I groan.

"Coming." I shout, before mumbling under my breath, "but not the fun kind."

Chapter Twenty-Four
CHARLOTTE

My palms are sweaty as I exit the powder room. I swear, I've had to pee a million times today. My heart rate picks up the closer I walk toward the conference room where I left Aiden and Thompson, my attorney.

After hashing and rehashing it, I decided to meet Preston and his legal team in person. Living with the man taught me that he will go through extreme lengths to get what he wants, but if I manage to make it seem like I'm giving in somehow, then maybe, just maybe, he'll give me this one thing. An uncontested divorce.

"You seem refreshed," a voice whispers behind me, causing my already erratic heartbeat to sputter. "Aren't you going to greet your husband, Charlotte?"

"You are *not* my husband. A husband doesn't treat their wife the way you treated me." Whirling around on him, my eyes narrow. "Distance *has* refreshed me. It's given me the clarity to see how toxic our relationship was. Never again, Preston. Never again will I let you control or mistreat me."

Preston's hand shoots out, gripping my wrist with bruising pressure. "This isn't over, Charlotte. Far from it."

"Everything okay out here?" Aiden's voice booms behind me and a sense of calm washes over me. Turning toward him, I see his eyes trained on Preston's hand, and by extension my reddening wrist.

Preston releases his death grip on me, placing both of his hands on his lapels and straightening his suit jacket. "Aiden." He walks past me and then Aiden without answering his question.

Aiden walks to me, where I'm still visibly shaking. "It's okay if you want to call this off. We don't have to do these negotiations in person."

"No. I refuse to let his actions control me. I'm no weak damsel. It's time he saw what I'm really made of." Chin held high, I take in a deep breath and walk my ass into the conference room. I meant what I said, it's time Preston met the real Charlotte Montgomery.

Beady eyes meet mine as I slip into my chair at the large oak table. Preston's attorney, Scott Mortimer, clears his throat. "Mrs. Rutherford."

I cringe at his use of my married name. "Please, call me Charlotte."

"Very well, Charlotte." He purses his lips before turning to my attorney, "Shall we begin?"

Thompson looks at me and I nod. "That would be a yes. What exactly does your client want? I thought the petition was pretty cut and dry." He produces another copy of the document and slides it across the table. "My client isn't asking for a dime other than what she came into the marriage with. You and I both know that she's entitled to an equitable division of the marital assets since there is no prenup. But instead of trying to fight for any of that, all she wants is for your client to agree to an uncontested divorce."

"She's lying. She needs me. She needs my money!" Preston's previously composed expression shifts into one of the monster I know all too well. He must be really angry if he's letting it come out in public.

Through my periphery I can see Aiden's hand clench under the table and I have to give him a small shake of the head. It isn't worth it to react. It will only make things worse and I want this over with as soon as possible.

"Do you see that?" Preston's eyes go wild as he looks between Aiden and me, pointing his finger and shaking it in the air. "They have a secret language."

Mortimer looks at his client, horrified. *Oh, that's right buddy, didn't know that's what lies underneath that bespoke suit.*

"Mr. Rutherford, if you'd please let me do the talking." Mortimer raises a brow, trying to get his client back in control.

Preston mumbles something unintelligible but settles back into his chair.

"Yes, we are fully aware of what's in your petition." Mortimer pushes the document back toward my attorney. "But my client is willing to give Charlotte half of the marital assets as well as the summer home in the Hamptons if she'd at least agree to marital counseling."

My mouth falls open. That's his family home. Why in the world would he even offer it up to me? I look at him, and for the first time I see a lost little boy in place of the monster I've grown accustomed to. My heart clenches, and a pang of guilt hits me straight in the chest.

"Charlotte, would you like a moment to think it over?" Thompson speaks softly as to not spook me.

My thoughts are all a jumble and my head is in a fog. It's not the damn house that has me so stirred up, it's the fact that he'd be willing to offer it to me, but for what? Counseling that won't work.

Looking at the man I married, my brows furrow, "Preston. I really don't think counseling will fix us."

"Please, Charlotte." He twirls the wedding band I gave him as his watery eyes look to me in supplication.

My chest feels like it's being ripped open, my heart being dragged out and slid across the table. Looking over at Aiden, I see his jaw is clenched and the vein on his neck is visible, the pulse beating rapidly.

"Char." Preston's voice snaps me back to him, and it's apparent that he caught me staring at my bodyguard. "Please. I'm begging you." His voice cracks and I know he must be desperate. In all my time with him, I've never heard him beg for anything to anyone.

Wringing the fabric of my skirt in my hands, I turn toward my attorney, "I need to think about it please. Can we reschedule this meeting, please?"

"Of course." Thompson turns to Mortimer. "I'll have my secretary reach out. How does a week from now sound?"

I nod and so does Preston, a precarious smile appearing on his pale face.

"Very well then." Thompson and Aiden get up from their seats, but I can't seem to move. I feel like I'm being weighed down by bags of sand, my mind still in a deep fog. "Miss Charlotte?"

Looking up at my attorney, I put on a fake smile. "Yes. Thank you for your assistance today."

"Of course, Miss." He extends his hand, pulling me out of my chair.

Finally braving a glance at Aiden, I see that all emotion has left his face. He is a blank slab of indifference and my heart plummets deeper into the pit of my stomach.

I need to fix this situation I've put myself in. This isn't fair to him.

Despite my wanting to reach out and grab a hold of his hand, I maintain my distance all the way to our SUV. Once inside, Aiden instructs the driver to take us to William's home.

Aiden keeps his eyes trained forward, not sparing me a glance, his indifference deepening the ever growing crater in my chest.

"Aiden." I hesitantly say his name in a whispered hush.

"No. There's nothing you need to tell me. Preston is your husband." His jaw clenches, the stubble covered skin flexing in the dim lighting of the car.

"I don't want to be with him," I rush out before I lose him forever. "In there, I just felt like I owed him something. Maybe a chance to explain why he's done what he's done. Maybe the counseling will help him see the error of his ways."

"Why? So he could be a better husband for six months only to return to beating you to a bloody pulp behind closed doors?" He finally turns to look at me, his rich hazel eyes piercing daggers into my soul.

"No, Aiden. I am not getting back with him. Under any circumstances and no matter what he promises." I blow out a breath, frustrated with this whole process. Frustrated with myself.

"Then why, Charlotte? Why give him hope?" His eyes narrow, but his voice drops, shifting from angry to hurt, and my heart clenches once again.

"He has issues. That much is clear. If going to therapy will help him see the light and get over whatever it is that's causing him to behave like a monster, then I'll have helped make him a better man. I promised him through better or worse, Aiden. I gave him my word." My hand raises to my chest, pressing into the skin and somehow trying to stop the deep ache I feel inside.

"That promise doesn't count when he's treating you like a punching bag, Charlotte." Aiden turns away from me and I feel like the cold night after the sun has stopped shining.

"No, it doesn't. I know that. I'm not stupid. But it still should mean something." A lone tear falls down my face, mourning the idea that Aiden and I could ever be a thing. "I think I owe him that much at least. Helping him through this."

Aiden doesn't respond, instead he takes out his phone and begins to type something on it. Before we know it, we're stopping in front of a massive skyscraper in downtown Dallas.

The driver gets out and opens my door, getting out I expect Aiden to follow me but he doesn't. Instead, William greets me on the sidewalk, directing me toward another car.

I'm about to turn back toward Aiden when the driver closes the door, shutting the man of my dreams behind it. My knees wobble and my hands wrap around my stomach as I dry heave.

What have I done?

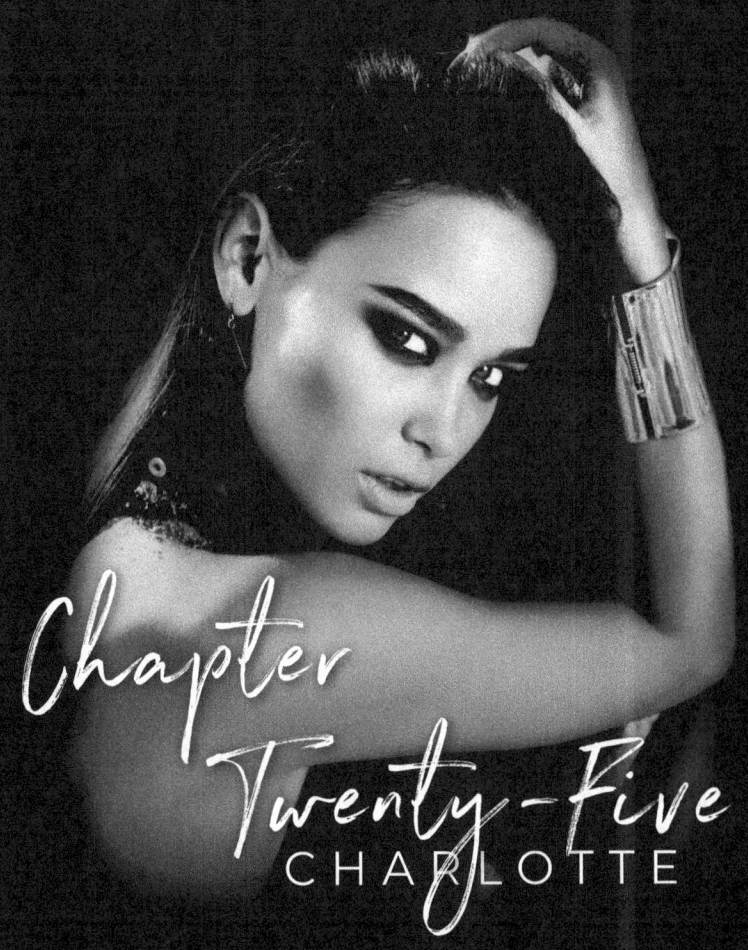

Chapter Twenty-Five

CHARLOTTE

The cotton of the sheets feels like sandpaper against my skin and no matter how many times I fluff the pillows, they feel like rocks. I'm restless and sleep will not be coming tonight.

I stared at the spot where the SUV stood for several minutes after it pulled away from the curb, waiting for this all to be some sort of nightmare.

It wasn't.

William silently waited by my side until I was ready to move. Not sure if he was actually being compassionate, or he just didn't want to get involved in my emotional clusterfuck of a life. Who can blame him, really? From the moment he met me, I've been nothing but a burden.

Letting out a growl, I fling my pillow across the room. I'm angry. Angry at myself, but also angry with Aiden. I couldn't be any clearer in letting him know that I didn't want to go back to Preston—that this wasn't me flaking on my feelings for him.

This isn't some cut and dry situation. It's messy and real. Nobody said divorce would be a cakewalk.

Taking in a centering breath, I let my lungs fill with cool air, hoping it'll do something for my frayed nerves.

The door creaks open and my breathing stops. Aiden's large form walks across the bedroom and toward his nightstand, pulling the drawer open and taking something out. My eyes follow him as he slowly makes his way back to the door without acknowledging me, making my blood boil and irritation spike.

"So that's it? You're just going to ignore me?" I spit out, forgetting any pretense of grace.

Aiden turns back to me, his shoulders slumped and eyes downcast, "I don't want to do this, Charlotte."

Those few words gut me, making my chest burn with the sting of a thousand knife wounds. Unable to hold back, a choked sob escapes me. "Aiden, I love you. I've always loved you. I choose you. Every time I choose you."

He juts his chin, the muscles along his jaw visibly flexing in the moonlit glow. "That's not what it sounded like this morning." Shaking his head, he brings his hand to his hair, running it through and tugging at the ends. "Look. It's not my place. You shouldn't have to choose between your *husband* and your lover. That's all sorts of fucked up and it's my fault for letting it get this far."

"But that's just it. I've always chosen you. Even when you were with my sister, you were always the one for me. Why can't you see that?" I fling the covers off of me and walk toward this statue of a man, my fingers reaching up and landing on his firm chest.

Aiden sucks in a breath, "Principessa. This is hard for me too. I want to respect you and give you the space to think things through clearly."

"But that's it. When it comes to you, there's no confusion. I don't think you understand. The counseling was not for the benefit of my relationship with Preston, but for the betterment of Preston as a person." My hands fall to his waist and I pull myself closer to him, needing his warmth to bring me comfort. "I never loved Preston—it was a marriage orchestrated by my mother—and since the man I really wanted was out of reach, I acquiesced. But even though I don't love him, I still promised I would care for him. Shedding some light on his actions, so that he can overcome them is the least I could do on my way out."

Aiden shudders under my hold, his strong hands grabbing hold of my arms and prying them free. "You don't owe him anything, Charlotte. That man set you free the first time he laid a hand on you. He shouldn't have the privilege of your help, much less sucker you into remaining his wife one second longer than necessary." He walks to the door, cracking it open before looking back. "But if you feel that's necessary, then I will respect your wishes. Until then, I think it's best if I keep my distance. Sleep well, little one."

As soon as the door shuts, my knees buckle and my body falls to the floor, tears flowing freely and pooling beneath me. As I lay on the hardwood floor, questions assault me, attacking everything I know and believe. But the most pervasive thought rings clearer and louder than the rest.

Will keeping my word cost me the love of my life?

Aiden

'Aiden, I love you.' Charlotte's words keep ringing in my head, like a broken record that refuses to let up.

The problem is, I love her too, but she's not mine to love. My principessa blindsided me with her sultry curves and big doe eyes, but it was her heart that won me over. Her heart and her fierce loyalty, even to those who don't deserve it, like Preston.

My fist slams into the punching bag, sending the massive piece of gym equipment swinging back.

"Care to talk it out?" William's voice rings out behind me, but I don't dare look him in the eye. He's a living lie detector and I don't want to hash out my fucked up feelings with myself, let alone my friend and business partner. "Okay, the silent treatment. How about you let me talk then? No objections? Okay, great."

As I grumble my displeasure, William walks the length of the gym until he's directly across from me, holding the punching bag steady. His aqua blue eyes meet mine, the edges crinkling as he smiles. "I get it, brother. Believe me. But love is love, and there's no sense in fighting it. You'll end up back where you were meant to and all you'll have done was waste precious moments with the woman you love."

I grunt, seeing the irony in my daughter's husband giving me relationship advice after I condemned their relationship from its inception. "Look, she's not mine to love. You know how I feel about infidelity. I've already crossed too many lines."

"She's yours in every way that counts. From what she's told Bella, she loves you. For fuck's sake, she's loved you since she was a little girl." His brows come together as he rubs the back of his neck. "You should have seen her on that sidewalk after you pulled away. It looked like she was grieving a death. You can't possibly look at her and think she has any feelings for that scumbag that abused her, do you?"

His words make sense, but I refuse to acknowledge them. "I still fucked up, man. She's *married*. I have been with a married woman. I-" I stab at my chest with my index finger. "the man who hates infidelity, am a fucking culprit, aiding a married woman in breaking her vows." Pressing the base of my palms to my eyes and rubbing, I groan. "I've become the very thing I hate."

Feeling a hand on my shoulder, I drop my hands and see William's lips pressed into a thin line. "Take it from me, life isn't all black and white. We don't exist in a vacuum of right or wrong, and trying to put your relationship with Charlotte in one isn't fair to you or to her." He offers me a tentative smile, patting my shoulder before releasing his grip. "You both have been through a lot. Hell, Charlotte is still going through her own version of hell, and she doesn't need you making her feel worse. In her own way, she thinks she's doing something honorable by helping Preston with his issues. The least you could do is be supportive of her."

"I *am* being supportive. I'm giving her space." I chew on the inside of my cheek, the words not sounding right, even to me.

William's brow raises, "Are you doing it to be supportive or are you doing it out of pride? From what Charlotte told Bella, she has no intention or desire to get back with Preston, and as far as I'm concerned, you're just wasting valuable time with the woman you love." William walks to the door, talking over his shoulder. "You should know better than anyone, tomorrow isn't promised. We live for the moment. We live for today."

His words hit home. I've seen so much death in my life, and he's absolutely right. All we have is the present.

Taking a towel off a chair, I wipe the sweat off my face and come to terms with what I know to be true. I love Charlotte Montgomery and I'll be damned if I let life steal another moment from us again.

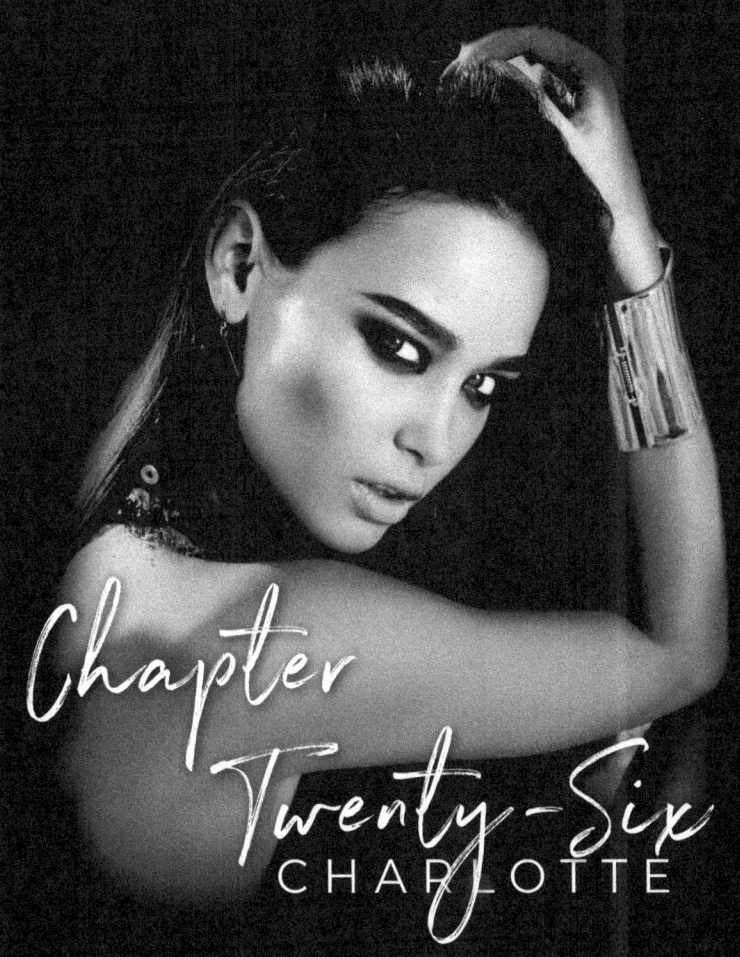

Chapter Twenty-Six

CHARLOTTE

The sound of a door creaking open pulls me from my nightmares.

My body is sore and my hair is plastered to the side of my face—a side effect of having cried myself to sleep on the cold hard floor. Before I'm fully awake, big arms scoop me up and press me into a broad chest. The scent of bergamot and cedarwood hits me, Aiden. My home.

His lips fall to my forehead, laying a gentle kiss atop the matted hair. "I'm sorry, principessa. I never want to cause you pain. It's my job to protect you, not cause you more sorrow."

He lays my body on the bed, my arms wrapping around his wide shoulders and pulling him down to me. "Stay with me."

"I'm all sweaty from my workout, let me shower first." His face splits into a breathtaking grin and my heart stutters.

"I like you sweaty." Batting my lashes, I flash him a coy smile, though I'm sure I look anything but cute right now. Puffy eyes from too many tears and crazy hair are not the least bit seductive.

His nose brushes mine, "If that's what you want, that's what I'll do."

His weight presses into me, covering me in a blanket of calm. "Yes, this is what I want. What I'll always want."

Aiden's lips find mine, brushing ever so softly back and forth. "Listen to me." His face pulls back and his eyes peer straight into my soul. "I love you, Charlotte Montgomery. I promise you this, I will always be your rock. Even if you don't need me, I'll be here for you. Every step of the way. I give you my word."

My breath catches, and the tears I thought had long left me resume their treacherous path down my face. "Aiden—"

"Shhh, baby. You don't have to say anything. Let me take care of you."

I nod, unable to come up with any coherent words. All I know is that the man of my dreams has just admitted that he loves me and he isn't going anywhere.

Aiden lifts the covers, tucking us both under their blanket of warmth and pulling me closer into his embrace.

Sinking deeper into his chest, I hold on for dear life. If this is some sort of dream, I don't want to wake up.

"Morning, sleepyhead." Bella's glowing face greets me as I step into the kitchen.

"Coffee, please," I mumble, unable to string together anything longer than those two words.

Bella chuckles as she points to the carafe behind her. "Just made a fresh pot. Call me a masochist, but I love the smell even though I can't have more than my one cup a day. And believe me, with how overprotective William is, I had to fight him for even that much."

I shake my head. If Aiden tried to take my coffee away, I'd strangle him. It's like my life source. This woman *does not* function without caffeine.

As I fill my cup, I realize what my subconscious has just acknowledged. Aiden is mine. He isn't going anywhere. He gave me his word and a Moretti's word is worth its weight in gold.

Then why can't I shake this sense of impending doom?

Letting that first sip of the magical black liquid slip past my lips, I moan. "So good." I whisper into my cup.

"Should I be jealous of the coffee?" Aiden speaks into the shell of my ear as his fingers float over my waist, gently caressing me.

Turning to face him, I give him a broad smile. "Maybe. It doesn't make me cry, you know."

His eyes narrow, the skin around the edges crinkling. "I promise I won't ever do that again." He lays a kiss on my nose and Bella giggles.

"You two are so adorable!" She beams up at us, not at all displaying any signs of discomfort at seeing her father with a woman other than her mother, and I for one am relieved.

Even though Aiden and I can't have a relationship out in the open, it's nice to know we have a place where we can be ourselves.

"What do you ladies have planned for the day?" Aiden pours himself a cup of coffee, leaving one of his hands on my waist.

"We have a spa appointment. It's only a couple of days until the wedding, so don't you be doing anything too dangerous, Dad. I need you in one piece so you can walk me down the aisle." Bella smiles, but even a blind man could see the concern etched across her face.

It's no secret she came close to losing her father this past year. That fear still runs through her today and I don't blame her, it runs deep within me too.

"No worries as far as I'm concerned. Titus and his team will be with you all day, meanwhile I'll head over to the team working at my home. We are installing extensive security measures so we won't have to crash here much longer."

"Finally! Not that I mind you guys being here, in fact I sort of love it." She purses her lips before continuing. "But it's about time you installed proper security in that house. It wasn't but a year ago that we had a crazy woman come into the home unannounced."

Aiden drops his hand from my waist and walks toward Bella, pulling her into his arms and squeezing tightly. "We had it under control, peanut. It would've gotten handled one way or another. But now that our family is growing, it's time we got more protection than just yours truly."

Bella's face lights up, her eyes going wide, "Oh my god, are you guys expecting?"

I spit out my coffee, spraying the black liquid all over the pristine white marble counters meanwhile Aiden chokes on his saliva. "No, Bella. I was referring to Charlotte. Our family is growing because Charlotte will be staying with us." He pauses, sucking in a breath as he turns to look at me. "Unless there's something you need to tell me..."

Taking a napkin, I wipe down the countertop at a feverish pace. "Nope. Nothing to share here. No babies in this womb."

Something flickers in his eyes, but it quickly disappears, leaving me wondering if he does in fact want a baby with me.

My heart flutters at the idea of our love creating something so beautiful, and in that moment I pray for it to be true. Maybe not in this instance, but definitely sometime soon.

Aiden turns back to his daughter, kissing her on the forehead before heading toward me and doing the same. "Okay, well now that that's straightened out, I'll be heading out. Call me if anything comes up. I trust Titus, but I don't want either of you feeling as if you can't reach me when I'm not with you."

"Yes, sir." Bella salutes her father as he walks out, meanwhile I blow him a kiss, mouthing that I love him.

Aiden winks, mouthing that he loves me too, making me beam like a damn fool. I'm lost for this man. Always have been and always will be.

"First comes love, then comes marriage." Bella singsongs as the door closes behind Aiden.

I give her the side-eye as I take the rag I'd been holding to the sink.

"Don't give me that look. I just call it like I see it." Bella snickers as she walks out of the kitchen. "Meet you back here in thirty! Massages and manis wait for no woman."

Laughing as I sip the last of my coffee, I can't help but grin. This is my new family and I finally feel as if I belong.

Despite the things I've endured, I'd relive them all willingly if they led me straight here.

I may've been born a Montgomery, but my heart will always be a Moretti.

Bliss. I'm in a sheer state of bliss as I exit the massage room. The therapist was able to work out some kinks I didn't even know existed. To say I feel like a blob of gelatin would be an understatement.

"Over here, Charlotte!" Cassie calls me from the hot tub in the center of the common area. This spa is amazing. All of the treatment rooms converge into a common space where there's a quiet area as well as a hot tub and plunge pool.

"Shhh. This is supposed to be a calming experience." Bella chastises her best friend while biting back a smile.

"Fine. No yelling. Anyway, you got here just in time. We're all asking the bride one personal question and she *has* to answer." Cassie moves over in the hot tub, leaving enough space for me.

I'm about to get in when I notice Bella isn't in the water and there's only room for one more. "Oh no, that's okay. Bella can go in instead of me."

Beaming up at me, she rubs her belly. "Thanks, babe, but I can't go in. It would be too hot for this nugget. But you could go in... unless there is something you haven't told us."

My entire body flushes at the thought. Unable to ignore the question any further, I recognize that I haven't gotten my period. My body goes from heated to ice cold in ten seconds flat, and it doesn't go unnoticed.

"Oh my god!" Ashley claps her hands excitedly. "Are you?!"

"I don't think so, but I'm not one-hundred-percent sure." Chewing on my bottom lip, I try to do some quick math in my head. It's only been a couple of weeks since Aiden and I first were intimate. Groaning into my hands, I let the girls in on my thoughts. "If I am, then it was a determined swimmer."

"Okay. I'm totally cool with you and my dad being a thing, but please never, and I mean *never,* talk about his swimmers." Bella visibly shudders and I can't help but giggle.

"Deal." Lowering myself to the ground, I sit next to Bella, submerging only my legs. "Better safe than sorry, right?"

"Right. And you all know what this means..." Ashley shoots me a toothy grin.

"Yes! More drinks for us!" Alyssa rushes to answer, only to have us look at her quizzically. "You know, because she can't drink like Bella?"

We all cackle, much to the spa attendant's dismay. "No, it means we are stopping by the drug store on the way home. We need to verify if she can in fact party at the wedding or if she will be partaking in Bella's virgin drink menu."

My chest begins to rise and fall rapidly, my head beginning to spin. What the hell was I thinking not using protection? I'm not even divorced yet, and what will my sister think? She doesn't even know Aiden and I are a thing.

"Breathe, Charlotte." Bella rubs my back. "It's going to be okay. Tell us what's going through your mind. You went from elated to freaked out in under a minute."

Unable to look any of the women in the eye, I drop my gaze to my thighs. "The first being the obvious, I'm going through a divorce. And the second, my sister doesn't even know about me and Aiden. I'm not sure how she'd even react to that, let alone our having a baby."

Ashley scoots over to my side, grabbing hold of my hand and patting it gently. "One thing at a time. First, we need to find out if this is even something you need to be considering. For now, let's enjoy the rest of the day in this amazing spa. Do you have a question for Bella?"

Face still heated, I look up at the woman that could very possibly become my daughter-in-law and go for broke, "Ready to call me Momma Charlotte?"

They all throw their heads back in laughter, the previous tension evaporating like the steam of the hot tub. Thank god these women understand my humor.

Yes. This is my tribe. I've found my family and I'm not letting them go.

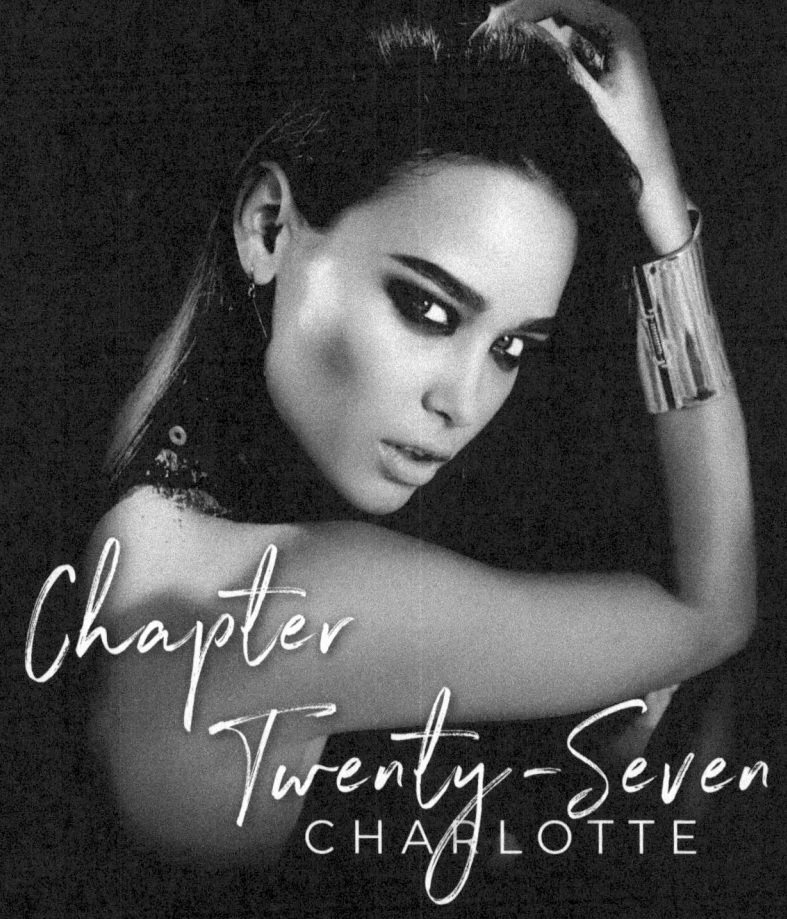

Chapter Twenty-Seven
CHARLOTTE

"**H**urry up and pee already!" Bella calls to me from the other side of the bathroom door.

"You rushing her isn't going to make her pee faster," Ashley teases. "Do you need some more water or juice?"

These ladies crack me up. "I'm about to open the door and let you ladies have a front-row seat if you don't stop asking me questions."

"Don't tempt Bella. She's crazy enough to do it. She might even hold the pee stick for you!" Cassie lets out a laugh as I hear someone smack her, presumably Bella.

"I will not. I'm just anxious to know if I'm going to have a little brother or sister." Bella pleads between fits of laughter.

Finally, I'm able to relieve myself, saturating the strip enough for it to start blinking at me. Thank goodness for digital tests.

I lay the plastic stick on the sink while I wash my hands as someone starts jiggling the lock.

"Open up. We know you're done peeing. I can hear the water running."

Opening the door, I see Bella standing there eagerly waiting. She doesn't even stop to look at me, but instead rushes over to the test and picks it up.

"Bella, that has pee on it!" Alyssa looks horrified as Bella waves the stick in the air, waving it toward her.

"I care for a toddler all day. That includes cleaning up all sorts of bodily fluids. If you think a little pee would scare me off, you're clearly mistaken."

I shake my head, laughing at the absurdity of this conversation. If you would have told me months ago that this would be my reality I would have told you you were delusional.

"So? What does the test say?" Cassie barges into the bathroom, attempting to pull the stick from Bella's hand.

"How about we let the potential mother-to-be look at the test first?" Ashley walks forward, taking the stick from a pouting Bella and hands it over to me.

I accept it, reaching out with a trembling hand. Taking in a deep breath, I look down at the little window, unsure of what I want it to say.

As soon as I see it, all uncertainty vanishes and I know that this is what my heart truly desires. Sucking in my lips, my eyes water and tears begin to fall freely from my eyes. "Pregnant."

The small room erupts into a cacophony of happy noises, a physical response to the joy I feel deep inside.

Bursting into our little bubble of estrogen, a male voice calls to us from the door.

"Everything okay?" Titus' body fills the doorframe, his curious smile looking at the lot of us.

I smile, quickly hiding the stick behind me. "Yes, just girl time. You know, talking about those pesky emotions you love so much."

"Aaaand that's my cue to leave. I thought y'all would have had enough of that at the spa. Apparently, I need to keep my distance at home too." He cocks a brow, his gaze falling on Ashley very briefly, something silent spoken between them before he steps back out. *Interesting.*

As soon as the bedroom door shuts, I turn to Ashley. "Okay, what happened to no secrets? I'm over here sharing a big moment with you ladies, meanwhile you and Titus are speaking code with your eyes."

Ashley sputters as Cassie bursts into hysterical laughter. "Oh my god, I can't believe you had the balls to call her out on something we've been insinuating all year!"

My cheeks burn, and I fear I might have really stepped in it this time. "I'm sorry, I thought it was so obvious. At least it seemed that way to me."

"Oh, trust me. It is. Even I noticed it." Alyssa's little voice chimes in from her position seated atop the bathtub ledge.

"Fine. The cat is out of the bag then, since you all claim to be all-knowing." She rolls her eyes as she lifts her hair into a messy bun. "It started right around when Aiden had his accident. I'd just broken up with my asshole of an ex."

"The one who cheated on you with his secretary?" Cassie asks, her mouth going slack.

"That would be the one. It started out as a revenge fuck but then turned into something else." She flails her hands in the air in obvious frustration. "Y'all know Titus. The man doesn't do relationships, so I don't even know what to call us."

My heart aches for her. I know what it's like to feel lost and unvalued. Before I can say anything, Bella puts in her two cents. "I say give him the cold shoulder. Stop giving him the cookie if he's not willing to commit."

"All in favor of Ashley withholding the cookie, say aye." Cassie rings out.

Unanimous 'ayes' fill the room before we all burst out into another fit of laughter.

Exhaling, Ashley raises her hands. "Now that my tragic love life, or lack thereof, is settled. Have you thought about how you're going to break the news to Aiden?"

All eyes fall on me and my stomach immediately wants to revolt. I'm not sure if it's the nerves or the little peanut. Seeing how it's so early, I'm betting on the nerves.

This is such a mess. I don't even know if he'll be happy and we're hardly in a situation where I could plan something special. "Oh god. I feel guilty for even wanting to celebrate such a special occasion when I shouldn't even be given this gift in the first place. I'm married to another man for fuck's sake." The women around me suck in a breath, no doubt surprised by my use of a curse word. But this moment calls for it. Hell, I feel like I belong on an episode of Jerry Springer. "How can I act like this is amazing news when the world around me is a mess and my sister... Oh my god, I don't even want to start down that road. She's going to hate me." I drop the stick into my lap and bury my face in my hands, unsure of where or how to hide from this shame.

"Don't freak out." Alyssa calls to me in a hushed tone. "If she really loves you, she'll understand. And if she doesn't, then forget her. You don't need her. You have us!"

"For someone so young, you're pretty wise." Cassie playfully shoves Alyssa before turning toward me. "The girl has a point. I'm not sure of the history between your sister and Aiden, but I've seen the way that man looks at you. You're it for him, and if that would've been the case with her and Aiden, then they'd still be together."

"I agree." Bella smiles at me, "And as far as the legal status of your relationship with Preston, that'll be over before your first checkup, if Thompson has his way. He's the best at what he does. So don't you worry one bit. There's no need to rush out and tell the world. We'll just keep it in the family until you're ready to share. Those who love you and truly know you will be supportive. In the words of wise Alyssa, forget them."

I feel a flutter in my stomach as I let her words sink in. I couldn't have asked for a better group of women to call my friends. No, not friends. Family. Looking up at my new tribe, I grin. "Alright. I think I know how I want to tell him."

Aiden

The house is quiet. A little too quiet. Pulling my phone out of my pocket, I check to see if Titus texted me an update while I was out.

Nope. Nothing.

What the hell? Is that a cinnamon bun on the ground? Holy hell, there's a whole trail of mini cinnamon buns leading into the hallway. My curiosity grows with every step I take, and when the path leads me to the stove, I'm at a loss for words.

There's a tiny note stuck to the oven. 'Open Me' is printed in feminine handwriting.

I reach for the latch, bringing down the door and reveal a massive bun in the oven.

Holy shit.

With shaking hands, I take it out and see the confirmation of what's been running through my mind since I left Charlotte this morning. My heart stutters and my whole body heats as I read the message written in the frosting.

'Baby Moretti Coming Soon'

I must stand there for more than a minute because Charlotte's hesitant voice repeats my name multiple times. Lifting my gaze from the bun in my hands, I see my beautiful woman chewing on her bottom lip as she shifts back and forth from foot to foot.

Dropping the plate on the counter, I rush to her and pull her into my arms. "Baby. A baby. What a blessing."

She lets out a breath as she trembles in my arms. "I was so worried you'd be upset."

Cupping her face with both hands, I tell her my truth, "How could I be upset at something that's a product of our love? I am not ashamed of you or of what we've created together. I love you, Charlotte. With every day that passes, I love you more and more. I couldn't think of a greater gift than the one you've just given me."

Her eyes peer into mine, soaking in what I've just admitted. "I love you, Aiden Moretti. And if being elated over this news makes me a selfish hot mess, then so be it." Her slender arms wrap around me, squeezing me tight. "This is all so surreal. It's like a dream come true. Well, minus the divorce and the whole sister's ex thing."

Her body shudders beneath mine, and I have to pull her back so I can see her face. "Hey, does that bother you? That I had a past with Clara?"

Chewing on the inside of her cheek, she hesitates before responding. "I'd be lying if I said it didn't."

I blow out a frustrated breath, I knew this would come up eventually. "Charlotte, she doesn't hold a candle to you. What I had with her was so insignificant it's never crossed my mind once since we broke up." Running a hand through my hair, I groan. "But you. God, I can't go a second without you popping into my head. It's all I do, constantly worry, wondering what you're doing, if you're safe. It's unlike anything I've ever felt. It can't be quantified or compared. You are on your own level, baby. There could never be another you."

Charlotte's eyes water as her little hands reach up to my face, pulling me down for a kiss.

As soon as our mouths come together, the world around us fades and it takes everything in me not to pick her up and throw her onto the counter, having my way with her right-the-fuck-now. Pressing my hips into her small frame, I moan. "*Principessa*, we need to take this to the bedroom or we're going to be giving the whole house a show."

"Yes, sir." Hand to forehead, Charlotte salutes before turning away and heading down the hall, her heart shaped ass swaying back and forth.

I follow her frame while shaking my head. This woman has me wrapped around her little finger and she doesn't even know it. *No problem.* I vow to show her I say what I mean, and I mean what I say. I'm not going anywhere, and anyone who has a problem with that is in for a rude awakening.

Charlotte Montgomery is *mine.*

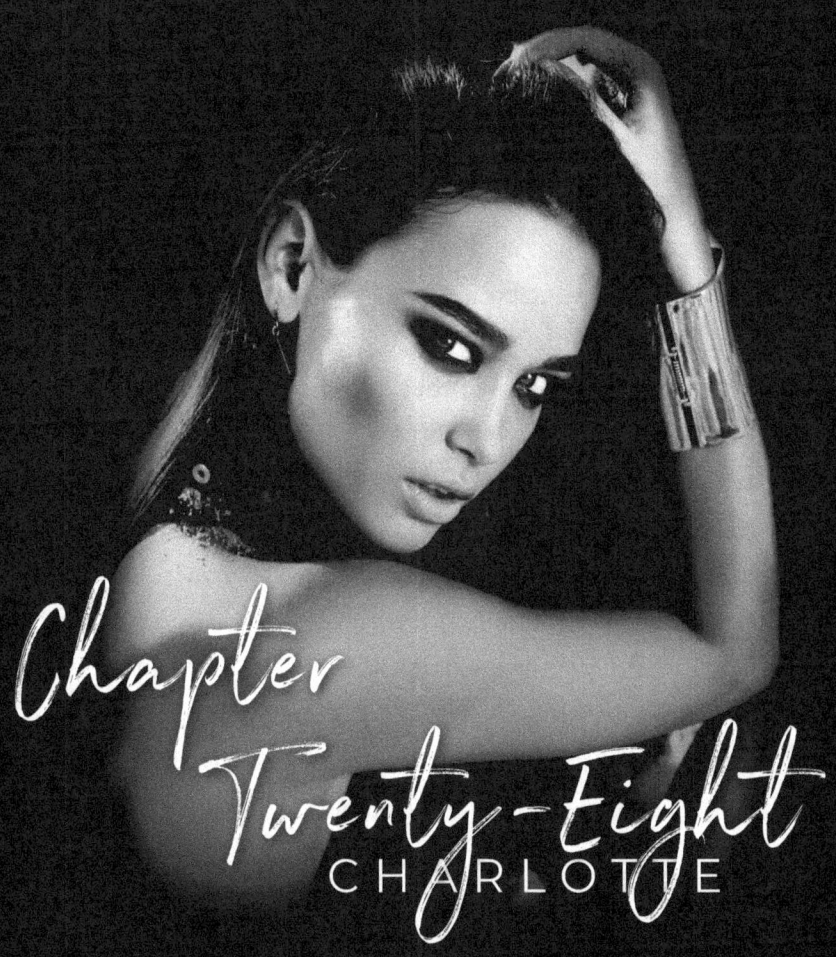

Chapter Twenty-Eight
CHARLOTTE

I t's finally wedding day and all of us WRATH ladies are in the family suite with Bella getting ready for her big day.

It's the first time I'll be out in public after having left Preston. So far there hasn't been a big scandal, but a small local paper printed their theories that our relationship was on the rocks. I laugh internally. *If they only knew.*

"You need to stop sweating. I'm not touching up your makeup, you know." The makeup artist, a friend of Cassie's is doing all the bridesmaids in soft shades of pink and plum. "I swear, you're sweating more than the bride."

Bella turns to look at me, concern written all over her pretty face. "Are you okay?"

"Yes, I'm perfectly fine. Don't you worry about me. It's *your* day.'" I clap my hands together and squeal. "You're finally going to be Mrs. William Hawthorne."

"I still think William should have taken your name." Cassie comments as she takes a sip of her mimosa. "Just saying."

"Oh, stop. We all know that if that's what Bella really wanted, that man would do it in a heartbeat." Ashley gets a distant look in her eyes as she sighs. "Ugh, if only all of the WRATH men loved that fiercely."

"Are you still withholding the cookie?" Alyssa giggles into her hands as Ashley turns the color of Bella's Louboutin heels.

"Leave poor Ashley alone." I call out, trying to end poor Ashley's embarrassment. I feel a strange pull toward William's sister and I hate to see her uncomfortable.

"Fine, I'll set my eyes on you. Are you ready to deal with the masses today?" Casie beams up at me, not knowing that she's just unleashed Dante's Inferno inside my mind.

Right on cue, my palms get sweaty and I feel a bead of liquid glide down my forehead. "It's time I was out in public. Besides, I couldn't be anywhere safer than at a wedding being guarded by the most elite security firm in the nation. And it's not like there will be paparazzi here, right?"

All the women look at each other as if they're in on something I'm not.

"About that..." Bella clears her throat, taking her sweet time to spit out whatever she has to say. "I agreed to let one magazine come shoot the wedding."

Cassie chimes in, seeing the color drain from my face. "It's one of the most anticipated weddings of the year."

I pull myself together, unwilling to let my fear of the media ruin this day for Bella. "Yes, of course it is! I'm glad you're having this special moment documented. And hey, it's not like I have a big sign above my head that says, 'Senator's wife, pregnant with lover's baby,' right?" I give an awkward laugh as my arms wrap around my waist.

With my fake reassurance, the girls go back to getting ready. Alyssa touching up her nails and Cassie supervising her friend doing Bella's makeup.

Ashley, however, plops down beside me in her pink monogrammed robe—Bella had one made for each of us and surprised us with them this morning as we arrived to get ready. Leaning in to me, she whispers, "It's going to be fine. All eyes will be on the bride, and if anyone says anything, we'll just tell them you're my plus-one." She extends her pinkie out to me in offering, "Deal?"

"Deal." I smile, taking her pinkie in mine and let out a long deep breath.

Everything is going to be okay.

Not okay. Not okay.

I spot my sister two tables away from the head table and she's staring at me slacked-jawed. Ren is giving his toast as the best man and I'm thankful for the time it's buying me. I know as soon as everyone begins to eat, she's going to approach me.

Making matters worse, Bella and Cassie seated me next to Aiden.

I see Clara's internal cogs spinning. Her eyes dart back and forth between an oblivious Aiden and me. If I thought I was sweaty before, I must look like I'm coming from the sauna right about now.

"Hey, you okay?" Aiden leans into me, whispering his question.

"Don't look now, but Clara is here and she's staring right at us." I manage to answer back without looking at him directly. I'm sure that Clara isn't the only one who's caught on to the fact that the senator's wife is seated at the head table, *sans* the senator.

Out of my periphery I see Aiden's eyes go wide, a rarity for a man who rarely shows emotion in public. "Okay then."

"Okay then." I reply, not saying anything else. I'm not trying to add more fuel to the fire.

As soon as Ren stops talking and the table begins to eat, I excuse myself, slipping past Bella and William, giving them both a kiss on the cheek and congratulating them once more and beelining it to my sister's table.

I'm not even five feet from her when her loud voice booms over all those seated with her, "Charlotte, what a surprise. I hadn't heard from you in so long and to find you seated at the head table no less." All eyes fall on me and I feel as if I'm about to stroke out. Pressing my nails into my palms I try to suppress the rage from her throwing me under the bus like this.

"Right. Well, a lot has happened since we last spoke." Turning to everyone around her table, I put on my best smile. "Hello, everyone. Please excuse me as I steal my sister away for a moment. I promise to bring her right back."

"Take your time." The man she's seated next to mumbles into his drink.

Clara purses her lips in displeasure, but she doesn't respond to his obvious dig. Instead, she puts on her mask of pleasantry and smiles at the others before getting up and following me to the ladies' room.

All that disappears as soon as the door closes behind us, and her mask falls, showing me the raging bitch that lies beneath. "So, you're into sloppy seconds, I see. Does Preston know?"

"Shh! Clara, watch your mouth." I chastise her as I lower myself onto the ground, checking the stalls for evidence of any occupants. Standing up once the room has been cleared, I turn back toward my sister. "I'm not with Preston anymore and you don't know what the hell you're saying."

"Oh, no. You don't get to play dumb here. He's my ex and never in the entirety of our relationship did he ever look at me the way he looks at you. I bet if you told him to walk on glass shards, he'd gladly do so." She releases a maniacal laugh, seemingly becoming more unhinged by the minute.

"Look, this is not the right time or place for this conversation, but if you must know, I love him." Shocked at the words that just came out of my mouth, I stumble a few steps back.

Apparently, Clara has the same reaction, so much so that she's stunned silent.

"Like I said, this isn't the time or place for this conversation. If you want, we can do this tomorrow or later this week."

"So you've been ignoring me all this time and I'm supposed to believe you'll just talk to me tomorrow as if you're not dropping the biggest bombshell of the century on me?" She slowly walks toward me, her eyes narrow slits of rage. "No, you don't get to call the shots. He was mine first."

Circling me, she continues her verbal assault and I brace myself for the daggers I know she's about to throw. "Say what you will, but I'm not engaging. I refuse to ruin this day for Bella."

"You'll leave this room when I'm good and ready." Clara pokes at my back with her index finger before continuing, "Here I am, the spinster sister, on a date with the least desirable bachelor in Dallas, meanwhile you throw away a catch with Preston only to go after *my* ex? Do you hate me that much?"

"I don't hate you, Clara. I love you. You're my sister. I only want the best for you."

A piercing cackle reverberates off the walls of the small room. "You're a liar too? Oh, this just keeps getting better and better."

"I'm not lying." Crossing my hands over my chest, I jut my chin, proud and strong. "I love you and I *do* want the best for you, even if you don't believe it. You can either choose to believe me and let me explain or you can shut me out, losing out on the only sister you have."

She steps closer, opening her arms for an embrace, the action catching me off guard since she still has murder in her eyes.

As soon as her arms are wrapped around me, she brings her mouth to my ear, "I'd rather die than hear you out. What you've done is unforgivable." She pulls away, pushing me before delivering her punishing blow. "I hope you're happy knowing it was my pussy he worshiped first."

I stand there slack-jawed at what just transpired. *I've lost my sister.*

She walks to the door, opening it wide and stepping out without another word. As the door clicks shut, my knees shake and my stomach revolts. Turning around, I hurl into the sink, a mixture of nausea and my nerves catching up to me.

I splash my face with water, groaning into my hands. *This couldn't have gone worse.*

"That was touching." A familiar voice startles me, causing me to whirl around and spray water everywhere.

"Michaela? What are you doing here?" My face heats as my mind races through all of the possibilities of why my husband's secretary could be at this wedding. "Is Preston here?"

"No, of course not. If you actually cared about the man, you'd know he's been a useless sack of meat. Unwilling to do his job, let alone get out for the social event of the year." She cocks a brow as she walks to the sink, turning on the tap to wash her hands. "I must say, it hasn't disappointed me yet."

"I don't know what you heard, but I'd appreciate you keeping my family business to yourself." Licking my lips, I try to sound as calm and confident as possible. "I know Preston wouldn't appreciate his dirty laundry being aired out. We're already expecting enough fallout from the divorce."

Michaela dries her hands with a towelette as she walks to me, patting me on the shoulder. "Don't worry, Charlotte. Your secrets are safe with me." Her fingers dig into me ever so slightly, and I have to wonder what has her so worked up. I've seen how Preston treats her. Hell, he treats the neighbor's dog better than he does her.

Shaking my head, I decide to give her the benefit of the doubt. What's done is done and there's no going back in time. "Thank you. We both appreciate it."

"Hmm." She hums as she walks to the door. "I'll see you around, Mrs. Rutherford."

Lifting my hand, I wave goodbye, but losing all semblance of being put together as soon as the door closes.

"What have I gotten myself into?" I whisper to no one, the empty room as full as my jar of confidence right now.

Smoothing my hair down and inspecting my makeup, I assess the collateral damage of my emotional outburst. Thanks to Cassie's friend and the use of waterproof makeup, my face is practically intact.

Giving myself a pep talk, I finally gather the courage to step back into the main hall. I'm about to open the bathroom door when a cleaning lady enters, pushing a large cart.

"Hello," I greet her while stepping around the cart, thinking I'm about to go find Aiden and let him in on the mess I've just been through.

Life, however, has different plans.

My body catapults forward, the organza from my dress tearing as it catches on something. I'm about to turn around when I feel the coolness of a wet cloth on my face. Struggling against the attacker, I manage to get a couple of good punches in, but whatever is on that rag is far stronger than me.

I put the last bit of energy I possess into kicking and biting, but it doesn't work. As the world starts to fade around me, I whisper one last word, the sweet name dying on my lips, "Aiden."

Chapter Twenty-Nine
AIDEN

I t's been over fifteen minutes, and Charlotte still hasn't returned from the restroom. Even Clara is back at her table.

Leaning over to Titus, I let him in on my concern before getting up and heading toward where I last saw her.

"Hey," Titus catches up to me and his face mirrors the concern I'm feeling. "Have any of our men alerted you to seeing anything suspect?"

"No, but after one of our men betrayed us by ransacking our safe house, I wouldn't put it past any of them to slip up."

There's a cleaning cart right outside the women's restroom which is concerning. This is a prestigious country club. Any cleaning would presumably be done prior to an event, behind the scenes, or if necessary, discreetly during a function like this wedding.

Off to the left is one of our men, running full speed toward me. "Aiden. I'm so sorry."

Those four words have my body turning into ice. "What. The. Fuck. Happened?" Each word comes out slow and deliberate as I try to control my temper from releasing a full-on shout of rage.

"Charlotte went into the restroom, her sister Clara and another woman both exited but she remained inside. Then a cleaning woman pushing a cart went in." His hand goes to the back of his neck, kneading it before continuing. "She came out a couple of minutes later and a maintenance man approached her, removing the white laundry bag from her cart and throwing it into a crate." He shifts on his feet, taking his sweet time in delivering the rest of the information.

"Just spit it out. We don't have all day and every damn second is crucial."

"One of our men went to inspect the crate, but before he could get a good look, the man apparently injected him with something. Alex was the one to find him on the ground and has him in a room recovering, but that's all the information we've been able to get out of him. As for our other men, they're going over surveillance footage, trying to find the woman or man. Charlotte has yet to be seen since having entered the bathroom. It's our theory that she was in the cart and then transferred to the crate."

"You think?!" I yell loud enough that people around us stare, but I don't give a damn. Charlotte is lost. God knows where, and this all happened on my watch. I shouldn't have let her leave the house, let alone bring her to a public setting like this. "Take me to our man. He has to have something that could clue us in as to who took her."

Titus' hand falls on my shoulder, squeezing in reassurance. "We will find her, brother."

We have to. I've just found her and there's no way in hell I'm letting her go.

Charlotte

A splash of water to the face has me jolting awake. "What the hell?!"

"There she is." A familiar voice answers. "It's about damn time."

Looking around the dark room, I try to find the bitch who drugged me. "Where am I, Michaela?"

I try to move but my hand and feet are tied up in front of me, it's a miracle I could sit up at all.

"Maybe you don't know who's in charge here. In case you haven't caught on, it's me, so stop with the sass. It will only make things worse for you."

Not giving a damn about her threats, I roll my eyes. "Spare me the drama and cut to the chase. What do you want and why did you do this? Is it money?"

"Of course you'd think that." She laughs in disgust as she steps into the light where a small lamp sits on a desk.

Looking around, I realize we seem to be in an office with very expensive art and furnishings. Are we still at the wedding venue? Trying to distract her, I try to get my bearings, eying any possible escape routes while continuing this conversation. "So if not money, then what?"

"You blind little bitch. Couldn't you see how good you had it? You had the man, the title, *and* the money. But did you appreciate it? No. You just made him worse. He's useless now. All he does is pine after your stupid ass." She presses the palms of her hands to her eyes and it's then I see the gun, the black metal surface glinting off the dim lighting of the room.

Well shit, maybe I shouldn't be poking the bear. It has a damn gun.

"I'm sorry, who are you talking about?" I have to ask because I'm at a loss for words. She couldn't be talking about—

"Preston, you fucking twit!" She shouts as I sit there, mouth hanging wide open. "I had him first. We had a good thing going and then you had to come along, the perfect little princess from old money. So prim and proper. The total opposite of me, a girl from Oak Cliff who worked her way up. But no matter how smart or how good I was to him, I was never enough."

"Michaela, I had no clue. I didn't know you two were ever a thing."

"Of course you didn't. I was the dirty little secret meanwhile, he took one look at you and knew you were going to be his trophy wife." Her body shudders in revulsion. "I even thought I could change his mind on your sham of a wedding night. But you must have some magical pussy because the four hours he spent with me did absolutely nothing to dissuade him from leaving you."

"You were with Preston on my wedding night?!" It's my turn to be disgusted. He'd been missing for a long time, and when he finally showed himself, he'd said it was because of work. Not wanting to fight with my new husband, I did what any obedient little wife would do—I shut up and didn't question him.

"Yes." She lets loose a diabolical cackle. "You. Are. So. Dumb. You never suspected a damn thing did you?"

My blood boils, and despite my predicament, I rip into her. "Don't be foolish, Michaela. Of course, I suspected, I just played the role. Behaved how he wanted me to behave. You're over here saying you wish you were me." I laugh hysterically, snorting at the ridiculous irony of this situation. "You wanted to be a puppet? Never having a word in anything, not even the clothes you wear or the friends you associate with. You are telling me that you wanted to cater to a man who beat you repeatedly because he was insecure, and constantly paranoid?"

"Yeah, about that..." Her face contorts, flinching at my words. "That's the part of the plan that didn't go as expected."

I blink slowly, trying to process what she just openly admitted to. "Excuse me?"

"Well, I might as well tell you since you won't live through this." My body freezes and the first inkling of real fear courses through me. Oblivious to my shift in demeanor, Michaela continues. "I wanted you to leave him, so I drugged him every damn day, hoping that his mood swings would drive you crazy."

"Michaela! Those were not mood swings. The man was paranoid and beat the shit out of me. Repeatedly!" I'm yelling so loud my throat stings from the strain on my vocal cords.

"Yea, that's the part that didn't go as planned. We had done coke before and it never resulted in violence. He would get paranoid but he never hit me, so I didn't think he'd do that to you." She cringes. Is she really trying to justify or apologize for her actions or Preston's behavior? "So, yeah. Whoops."

"Whoops? I slipped some coke in his drink, whoops? It's my fault he's going crazy and beating his wife, but I'm going to keep drugging him?"

"Oh no, sister. I stopped drugging him once I saw it wasn't doing a damn thing to make you leave. You're the stupid one for staying as long as you did. It's been over a year since I gave him his morning joe with the Michaela special. Everything he's done since has been because he's so psycho obsessed with you. I've had to live with this shit for so long, only for you to go ahead and ruin what little I had left of him when you left."

"Are you saying you still had him during our marriage?" My stomach rolls and I'm about to vomit, my mind immediately falling on the baby. The poor innocent baby that doesn't deserve to die in this office in god knows where. "Look, you can have him. All of him. He's not mine nor do I want any part of his obsessive abusive personality. Just let me go and I won't tell a soul."

Laughing maniacally, Michaela begins to pace in front of me, her face going in and out of the dark like some evil villain in a movie. Fitting.

"You don't get it. You broke him." She waves her gun in the air, waving the tip around in a circle. "The man won't go to work.

Won't shower unless I drag him. Won't even eat without my having to force feed him. Seems to me like I'm doing your job and getting none of the credit. Meanwhile, you go off gallivanting with your bodyguard, leaving me to clean up your mess."

"My mess?!" I screech so loud it hurts my own ears, but I can't help it. "You are delusional. You two had an affair before and during our marriage. You drugged him and stood by watching as he abused me. Then when I finally gather the courage to leave that toxic relationship, you have the balls to kidnap me and blame me for the sick and twisted mess of a relationship you two have." I close my eyes, shaking my head while rolling in my lips. "Nope. Not it. That craziness is all on the both of you, not me."

My eyes are still closed when the back of her hand connects with my cheek, sending my head swinging in the opposite direction.

Turning back to look at this lunatic, I see her other hand is raised, the barrel of her gun pointed straight at me. "You don't get to tell me that, you ungrateful little—"

The window behind Michaela shatters, little pieces of glass flying into the room, shooting around her like a halo of destruction. Like a perfectly orchestrated moment, she pulls the trigger as men fly in through the window.

I try to yell, but my breath catches and my chest burns. Looking down at my hand, I see crimson liquid seeping through the bodice of my dress and onto my pale skin.

God, no. The baby.

My vision blurs into a white fog as reality slips through my blood-stained fingers.

My baby, my poor baby.

A numbing ache comes over me as wetness falls from my eyes and I lose the last grip of hope I once held.

This is it. This is our end.

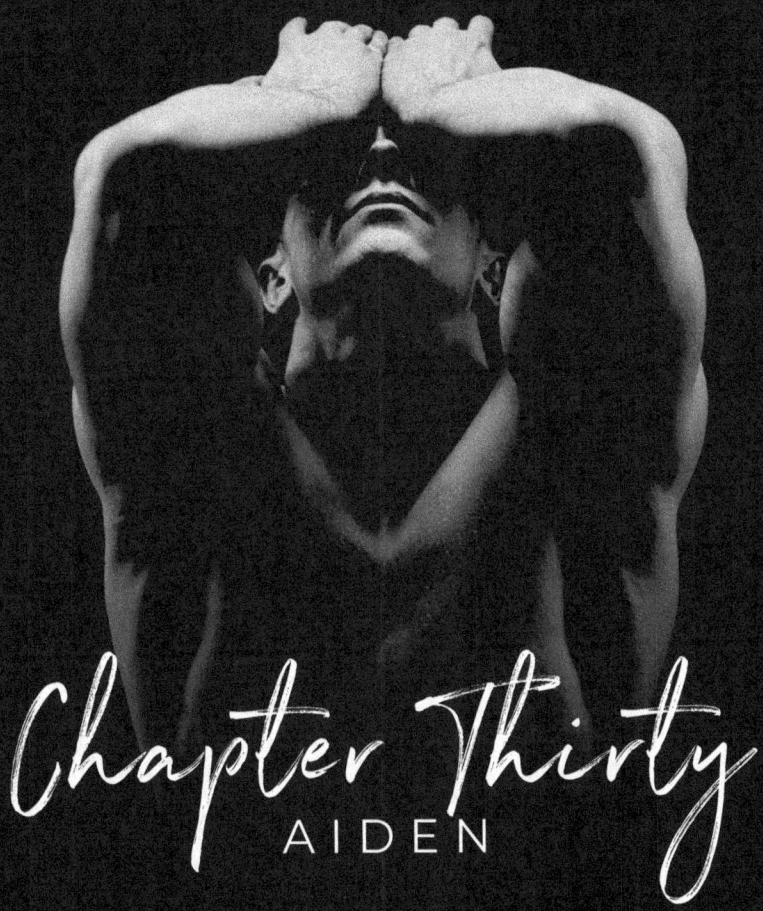

Chapter Thirty

AIDEN

"**Y**ou need to wait, man." Titus puts his hand on my chest, holding me back from charging through that damn window like a Neanderthal, ready to take his woman home.

Half of my men as well as a team of medics are all outside the club's main building, with the other half of our detail on the inside—all awaiting orders.

Thankfully, the orchestrator didn't take Charlotte far.

We were able to follow the crumbs to an office where Michaela has Charlotte holed up. Why Preston's secretary would want to hurt Charlotte is beyond me, but whatever the reason, I'll make sure she's taken care of.

Michaela had paid off a maid and maintenance worker to do all of the heavy lifting for her so she'd have an alibi during the kidnapping. Unfortunately for her, the two were still on the premises and sang like a canary as soon as we caught them.

The audacity this woman has to take Charlotte right from under our noses is infuriating. She had to know we'd find her right away.

My chest vibrates with pent-up emotion, about to boil over and unleash its wrath onto all those that get in my way. "How can you ask me to wait when she's in there? My child is in there!"

"Child? She's pregnant?" The look of shock on Titus' face matches that of everyone else around us. "Aiden, we had no clue. Congratulations."

"Why are you congratulating that asshole? I'm the father. That's *my* wife he's talking about." A voice to my right catches me off guard and I see two of my men holding on to Preston's arms, keeping him from going anywhere.

Charles, one of our senior men, speaks up first. "We found him lurking around outside, trying to find a way into the wedding. What do you want us to do with him, boss?"

Walking closer to Preston, I make my intentions known. "Charlotte is my woman, and our baby will never know you or the toxicity you spew. You are a disgrace of a man and if you come near either of them again, I will make it my life's mission to destroy you." Turning back to Charles, I cock my head. "Take him to the holding cell. I think he needs a little reassurance that we mean what we say."

"Yes, sir." Both men drag Preston away kicking and screaming, but one thing he says has my whole body going rigid.

"That baby is mine. Legally. It's mine and I will never relinquish my rights!" An evil glint flashes in his eyes, and I know he's telling the truth.

I know the baby is biologically mine, we've done the math— not that I'd care either way—but since she's still married, the law will consider him to be the father.

Unfortunately for him, he's dealing with a Moretti and we don't back down.

He won't take my woman and he definitely won't take my baby.

"It's time. We need to act now." Titus' voice shifts my focus back to what's important. Keeping Charlotte and the baby alive.

There are men on the inside, ready to break down the door as we enter through the exterior.

Giving our men the word, we shatter the window and throw in a flash grenade, awarding us the upper hand as we move forward.

As soon as my feet touch the ground, I see her. My beautiful Charlotte crumpled on the ground, surrounded by glittering shards of broken glass and swimming in a pool of crimson.

"Noooo!" I run toward her lifeless body, not caring that my men have yet to secure the bitch that did this to her. Immediately cradling her to my chest, I try to bring her back to me. "Talk to me, baby. Tell me you're okay."

The team of medics finally make their way inside and try to pry her from my grasp. "Sir, you have to let us care for her."

Reluctantly, I release her, knowing that they are better equipped to handle this type of situation than I am at the moment.

My brain is a jumbled mess of anger, fear, and overwhelming love. I love this woman more than I ever thought possible. And here I am, about to lose her.

"She's got a pulse, but it's weak." He begins to lift her onto a stretcher as another person applies pressure to her wound. "We need to transport her immediately, sir. Will you be coming with us?"

"Yes." I grunt, the onslaught of emotions too great for me to be able to say any more. My eyes sting and my chest tightens as I follow the stretcher out to the emergency vehicle.

I don't care to look back at Michaela. I know Titus and the others have the situation handled and there will be time to deal with her directly. For now, all that matters is Charlotte and our baby, but this is far from over.

Those that have threatened what's mine will pay, and they will rue the day they crossed me.

Charlotte

The scent of coffee has me stirring in my sleep. *Mmm*, coffee. Peeling my eyes open, I see that I'm not home.

White sterile walls surround me and beeping monitors are positioned to my left and attached to my arm.

Bolting up in the bed, I frantically look around, trying to make sense of everything.

"Whoa there, princess." Aiden places his hands on my shoulders, trying to lower me back onto the bed. "You need to rest. You've lost a lot of blood and need to take it easy."

A whimper to my right has me turning, and what I see shocks me. Clara clutching a cup of coffee as her tear-stricken face looks at me with so much pain. "I'm so sorry, Char. I didn't mean any of the things I said before. This is all my fault."

I reach out for her hand, squeezing it tightly when our fingers intertwine. "Shh, it's okay. I love you, Clara."

"I love you too, Char. But this really is all my fault. I told Preston where you were."

I feel Aiden tense behind me, his body rising from its place. "What do you mean you told Preston?"

Chewing on her lower lip, Clara comes clean. "That time you called me? I was so angry. I'd heard Aiden's voice when he said he'd ordered from Tyler's. I felt so betrayed. I didn't think." Her fingers tighten around the cup she's holding and her eyes focus on the black liquid as if it were the most fascinating thing on earth. "Aiden had mentioned having ordered from Tyler's. Well, there's only one Tyler's in the entire metroplex. I ran to Preston and told him what I knew, not even taking into consideration what that could have meant for your safety."

"You little—" Aiden is about to jump over the bed, when I place my hand on his chest.

"Stop. She's sorry." I look into his stormy eyes, ready to go to battle for me, and my heart melts all over again. *I love this man so much.*

"That doesn't justify it, and we aren't done here, but for the sake of your recovery I'll let it go. For now."

"Thank you." I pull his hand toward my mouth, placing a gentle kiss on his palm before turning back to my sister. "Clara, I forgive you. We're family and despite everything we've been through, I know you'd never wish me physical harm."

Placing her coffee on the floor, she gets up and pulls me into a hug, her arms shaking as they wrap around me. "I truly am sorry. I love you, little sister."

"Gentle. She just got out of surgery and we don't want to disturb the incision." Aiden rumbles, but it's his words that give me pause.

"Surgery?" My hands release Clara and fly straight to my stomach, my heart beating so hard I feel as if it's in my throat. "The baby?" My voice cracks as Aiden's lips roll in.

Shaking his head, he answers, his voice thick with emotion. "No. I'm so sorry."

The room spins, my vision goes dark, and my heart drops into my stomach. Never in my life have I experienced such excruciating pain. It feels as if my chest were caving in, swallowing my soul and leaving behind a dark hole, never to be filled again.

Releasing a piercing screech, my hands clutch on to my stomach, trying to wish this all away. *This can't be real. This can't be my life.*

Aiden wraps his strong arms around me, "Let it out, *principessa*. Let it all out." Stroking my hair, he presses his lips to the top of my head. "I promise you, we will make her pay. We will avenge our child."

Burying my face into his chest, I hang on to him for dear life, my anchor in this sea of despair. As I feel sanity slipping away, I let his words ring through me.

We will avenge our child.

Clinging to those words like a prayer, I vow to make them my truth. Those words and Aiden's arms are the only solace bringing me any sense of comfort. Letting me fall deep into him, I let go, crying until every tear has spilled from my eyes and my body has run dry.

Disoriented and unaware of how much time has passed by, I finally look up, my tired eyes meeting those of my love's.

"I'm ready. Let's go make her pay."

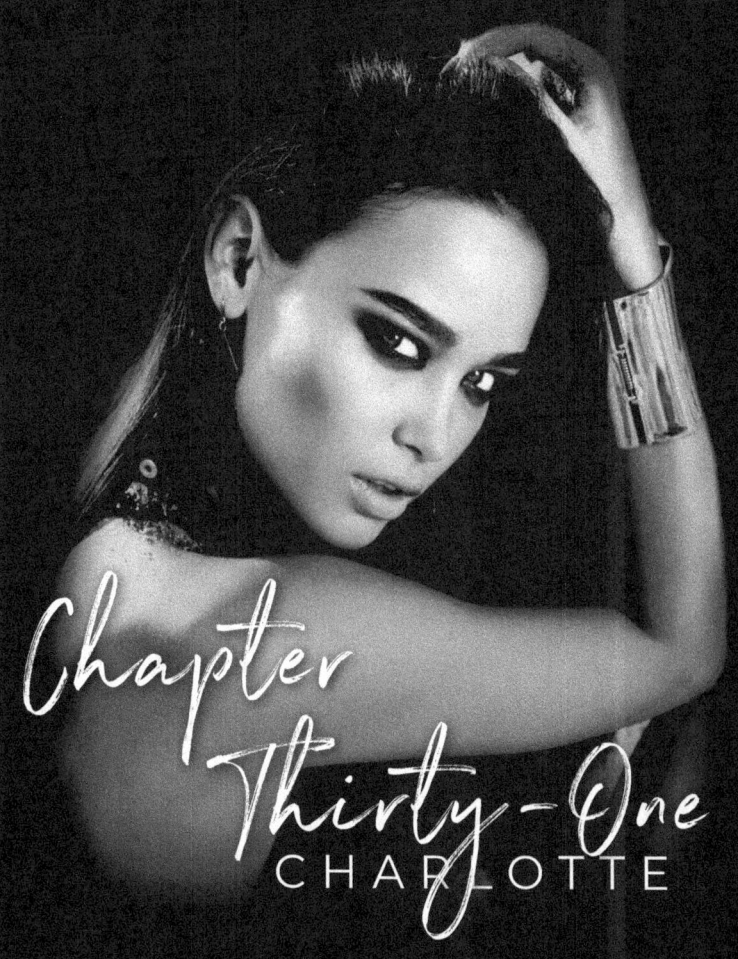

Chapter Thirty-One
CHARLOTTE

*F*ive Months Later...

Staring into the lifeless eyes of my ex-husband, I feel nothing but disgust.

It's been months since the loss of my baby's life, and to say that I've moved past the grief and heartache would be a blatant lie.

Yes, seeing Preston's face as the judge signed our divorce decree was satisfying. And yes, watching Preston and Michaela being carted around in an orange jumpsuit did make my lip twitch in an almost smile—but not one day goes by where I don't mourn

Despite time failing to bring me any peace, it has brought me one thing. Clarity.

These two monsters sitting in this courtroom are the epitome of what is wrong in our world. It was their narcissistic, selfish, and destructive behavior that caused this tragedy—and I'm here to make sure they pay for every second of pain they've inflicted.

A door opens behind the stand and a white-haired man in a black robe enters the room, ready to deliver the jury's verdict. It's been a long and painful road to where we are now, with so much deceit being unearthed.

The least shocking of all was finding out that Preston was the one behind the kidnapping. He'd enlisted Michaela's help, but to his dismay, she had her own plans. Wanting vengeance, she deviated from their plan and hauled me into an office instead of delivering me to Preston who'd been waiting out in the parking lot.

My hand flies to my chest as Aiden's hand rubs gentle circles on my back, trying to soothe the sharp pain that's become a constant companion to my life.

"All rise," the bailiff calls as we all stand, waiting as the judge takes his place behind his gavel.

"You may be seated." Clearing his throat, the judge looks at the file in front of him before his eyes fall on the wretched duo in the orange jumpsuits. "The Court has reviewed the verdict and finds it in order. Defendants and counsel, please rise."

Both Preston and Michaela as well as their counsel stand up, facing the panel of jurors who will issue their finding.

Once everyone is situated, the judge instructs the jury. "Foreperson, please go ahead and read the verdict."

"Yes, your honor." A middle-aged woman with short brown hair stands tall, both of her hands tightly gripping on to the piece of paper in front of her. "We the people find the defendants Michaela Rodriguez and Preston Rutherford, guilty of aggravated kidnapping under section twenty of the Texas Penal Code."

The whole room bursts into loud chatter while the judge brings down his gavel, trying to silence the room, and letting the woman continue only once everyone has quieted down.

"We the people find defendants Michaela Rodriguez and Preston Rutherford, guilty as to the charge of murder under section nineteen of the Texas Penal Code."

The whole room erupts into even louder chatter, and the judge is forced to bang his gavel once more. "Order in the court, or I will force everyone out."

I understand the reasoning behind the uproar. Texas is one of twenty-nine states which allows murder charges for the death of an unborn child. It can be quite controversial to some, but in my eyes, it's justice.

These two don't get to walk away with a simple two year sentence for kidnapping. No. They deserve to face the full extent and wrath of the law.

I cling to Aiden as the judge issues further instructions to defendants' counsel regarding phase two of the proceedings, where sentencing will take place. Thanks to the guilty verdict for the charge of murder, they each face up to ninety-nine years in prison.

Aiden's arm wraps around me, holding me tight. His tears wet my face as he places a firm kiss on my forehead. "For our baby."

"For our baby." Closing my eyes, I bury myself deeper into him, letting my face rest in the crook of his neck.

Knowing that Preston and Michaela have had their lives destroyed and will be sentenced to prison brings me a little solace, but nothing this court could provide would ever bring our baby back.

There's a hole in my heart that will never be filled, a void that will forever belong to a life that never touched this earth.

My little angel.

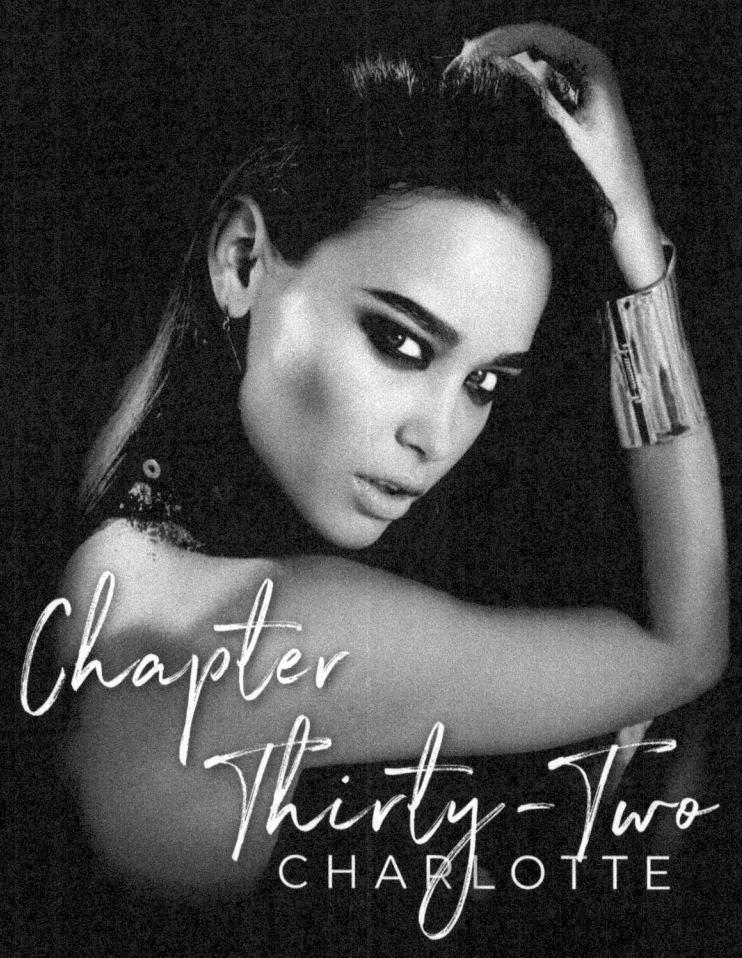

Chapter Thirty-Two

CHARLOTTE

Three months later...

    I stare out into the garden, looking at the beautiful leaves turning orange and red. Fall is upon us and I'm excited to have some holiday cheer injected into our home.

    I've officially moved in with Aiden and the twins. However, Nanny Sylvie isn't with us any longer since she decided to help her family with her own grandbaby.

    A baby. My heart squeezes, remembering our loss. It's been eight months since the tragic incident, but it feels as if it were just yesterday.

I don't think the ache will ever go away, even despite Preston and Michaela each receiving a sixty-four-year sentence for their transgressions.

My hands fall to the new life growing within me, an unexpected blessing through the darkness of this year.

Aiden and I found out we were expecting last month, and we've yet to tell everyone, despite my friends' suspicions. Those women can smell out a secret a mile away, but I'm still not ready to come clean. It doesn't feel real yet. Like I'm waiting for the other shoe to drop, tearing yet another life away before it's had the chance to flourish.

"What's going on in that pretty head of yours?" Aiden's body wraps around me like a soothing blanket of warmth, his arms engulfing me from behind as his lips land gentle kisses on my neck.

"The same as always." I turn my head, looking into his mesmerizing hazel eyes.

Our noses rub, letting me feel his breath on my lips. His scent has become a synonym to comfort and seduction. I count my blessings, thankful for this man who's helped me hold it all together.

"The boys and I have a surprise for you." His strong hands rub down either side of me, caressing my arms. "Why don't you follow me?"

"Should I be concerned? The last time you all had a surprise for me, I had to replace my entire book collection." I shake my head and laugh at the memory of the boys trying to make me a bookshelf for my classics, only to have painted over the books themselves.

"No paint was involved in the making of this surprise. Besides, I was there to oversee it." He gives me a warm smile, his dimples coming out to play and melting away all remaining sadness in my disposition.

I love this man with all of my soul. I truly couldn't be more blessed.

Aiden pushes open the door to the game room where Matt and Max stand in black shirts that say '*BLING PATROL.*'

Okay...

"Sit with us!" Matt runs up to me, tugging my arm.

"We have a game for you to play." Max shoves a controller into my lap as I sit between both boys.

Pushing the little round start button on the controller, the television comes to life before me. There's a beautiful princess with flowing dark brown hair, moving forward through a dark swamp. Suddenly, two little boys join her on her quest, fighting off ghosts and ghouls.

Coming into a massive clearing, a banner falls over the screen as a prince rides in on a horse.

Oh. My. God.

My eyes sting with the promise of tears as I read the message written just for me:

You are the hero of your story.

You are the strong knight your soul called on to survive.

You are the powerful woman we want by our side.

Charlotte Montgomery, will you do us the honor and join our tribe?

Dropping the controller, both hands fly up to my mouth as I gasp for air, my chest tightening and my vision blurring as tears flow freely down my face. This moment couldn't be more perfect if I dreamed it up myself.

Looking down in front of me, Aiden is down on one knee with either boy to his side, his own eyes glossy with unshed emotion. "What do you say, Char, will you marry us?"

"Yes, yes. A million times yes!" Hurtling myself off the couch and onto Aiden, I extend both arms out, engulfing the boys in one massive hug.

From day one, this has been my family, only now it will be official.

Not ten minutes ago, I'd just said I couldn't be more blessed. God, I was so wrong. This right here is far beyond any blessing I could have imagined.

As we continue to laugh and hug it out, I'm reminded that these moments in life are the ones worth holding on to. The ones I will cherish for all eternity.

Love.

Family.

Friendship.

The secrets to a life worth living.

MEN OF WRATH SERIES (forbidden love):

ACTS OF ATONEMENT
age-gap/nanny/single dad

ACTS OF SALVATION
age-gap/best friend's uncle

ACTS OF GRACE
Brother's best friend

ACTS OF MERCY
age-gap/stepbrother

MAFIA ROMANCE:

OMERTA: A VERY MAFIOSO CHRISTMAS
Mozzafiato, prequel to MAGARI

MAGARI
Capo dei capi falls for an outsider

Let's stay connected. I'd love to hear what you thought of the book, what's on your TBR list, or simply how your day is going.

www.EleanorAldrick.com

Instagram
@EleanorAldrick

Goodreads
www.Goodreads.com/EleanorAldrick

Twitter
www.Twitter.com/EleanorAldrick

Facebook
www.Facebook.com/EleanorAldrick

Acknowledgments

This is always the hardest bit for me to write. Not because I'm ungrateful, but because there are so many and so much I'm thankful for that it would probably be enough to fill another book.

As always, first and foremost, I'd like to give a shout out to my real-life Prince Charming. I am beyond thankful for my husband. I've been blessed with a man who is truly supportive in every sense of the word, not complaining one bit as I pour myself into my books and create these stories for you. Love you babe, you're the real MVP.

I'd also like to acknowledge my dear friends who have carried me through moments of self-doubt, always helping me push forward and be the best version of myself. I am truly grateful for you Domino, Kellie, Taralyn, Julie, Tracy, Dana, Sara, and Ande. I love you all, to the moon and back; and even though I'm not always the most expressive person in the world, know that I appreciate you.

A massive thank you is also in order to all my beta and ARC readers. I appreciate all of your feedback and your desire to help my book baby be the best version of itself. Acts of Redemption wouldn't be what it is today without you.

Another chapter of gratitude goes out to all of the bookstagrammers that have helped share all of the graphics and teasers for AOR. I love seeing all of the edits and hype for my babies, knowing you're just as excited as I am means the world to me.

And last but not least, you, the reader. Thank you for taking a chance on my books and letting me into your imagination. I hope you truly enjoyed the ride, and if you did, I'd be extremely grateful if you left my book a review.

XoXo,
Eleanor Aldrick